Tearjerker

ALSO BY DANIEL HAYES

Kissing You

Tearjerker

—◖◗—

A NOVEL BY

Daniel Hayes

Graywolf Press
SAINT PAUL, MINNESOTA

Publication of this volume is made possible in part by a grant provided by the Minnesota State Arts Board, through an appropriation by the Minnesota State Legislature; a grant from the Wells Fargo Foundation Minnesota; and a grant from the National Endowment for the Arts, which believes that a great nation deserves great art. Significant support has also been provided by the Bush Foundation; Target, Marshall Field's and Mervyn's with support from the Target Foundation; the McKnight Foundation; and other generous contributions from foundations, corporations, and individuals. To these organizations and individuals we offer our heartfelt thanks.

MINNESOTA
STATE ARTS BOARD

NATIONAL
ENDOWMENT
FOR THE ARTS

Published by Graywolf Press
2402 University Avenue, Suite 203
Saint Paul, Minnesota 55114
All rights reserved.

www.graywolfpress.org

Published in the United States of America

Printed in Canada

ISBN 1-55597-409-0

2 4 6 8 9 7 5 3 1
First Graywolf Printing, 2004

Library of Congress Control Number: 2004104189

Cover design: Scott Sorenson
Cover photograph: Daniel Hayes

For Monk
With big, big love

Everyone carries a room about inside him. This fact can even be proved by means of the sense of hearing. If someone walks fast and one pricks up one's ears and listens, say in the night, when everything round about is quiet, one hears, for instance, the rattling of a mirror not quite firmly fastened to the wall.

Franz Kafka, *The Blue Octavo Notebooks*

I
—◄O►—

The first story I ever wrote was "How the Dog Got Its Tail."
Writing was easy then. The contents of the story aren't impor-
tant. Suffice it to say that I was a child at the time; oblivious
to career aspirations, living in the nowhere of Appleton, Wis-
consin, I was writing to answer questions for which I could find
no conventional answers. Honestly, I can't recall the specifics—
something about happiness, a way of expressing it without hav-
ing a mouth that could smile. But I do remember going into the
garage and cutting two pieces of wood, filching a couple of brass
hinges, and making a cover that was sturdier than the covers of
the books on the shelves in my bedroom. And I worked hard on
decorating the cover. I can't remember exactly how I illustrated
it—with a dog and a tail that was attached? Detached? Little
dots indicating its recent attachment?

The story was important, of course, but more important
was the book as object—a rectangular entity that resembled the
ones I already owned. Even then I resented my status as passive
reader, starstruck consumer. Already the satisfaction of feed-
ing on words must've been wearing a little thin. And so I was
writing my own book, the purveyor of fantasies and not just their
silent witness. Given the choice of wielding the spoon or meekly
opening my mouth, I knew what I wanted.

UNTIL I BOUGHT ONE, I'd never touched a gun, never stood in front of a full-length mirror pointing a gun at myself. *Bang, bang.* Mine was a Magnum .357 purchased in New Jersey, much more handsome than I'd imagined a gun could be.

A gun was tantamount to a secret, I realized soon enough; it required the right coat with a pocket roomy enough to provide a hiding place. A gun was also an instrument of illusion; it had a way of fudging the difference between appearance and reality. In the small town of Sandhurst, New York, where I lived, I probably seemed like just another man taking an evening's stroll through the neighborhood, wearing a long, olive-colored gabardine coat. But was that really the case?

I made a habit of taking such walks, working against the initial trepidation—the fear that danger might approach if only to create a situation apropos of my secret. There was also a worry about the gun going off and sending an excruciating shot toward my groin. But eventually, as I went walking past the lit windows, peering in for a peek at the familial bosom of my anonymous neighbors, fear gave way to courage. I found myself falling into an almost dreamy state—just this side of serenity. It made me think of prayer, meditation, afternoon naps. It made me think of the attractive nurse who gave me too much codeine for a third-degree burn to my hand when I was seventeen.

There were nights when I'd return to the house and stand in my kitchen and stare down at the gun, asleep in the palm of my hand. It lay there like some solemn bird with one eye shut, feigning death—quiet and yet very, very powerful. It held its breath with the best of them. Who knows, maybe I was fooling myself, but I sensed—in the sheer weight of the weapon—a gravity, an authority beyond my own. Was I wrong?

— —

How's the bed?

Robert Partnow lifted his head and looked in my direction. Fine, he said.

I see you've chosen the lower berth, I said. Smart choice.

Should I be expecting company? he said—his eyes rolling upward.

No, no. IKEA just had a fantastic deal on bunk beds. I couldn't resist. You slept well?

I didn't sleep well. I barely slept. I have a headache.

And this when you can afford to sleep, I said—shaking my head. How many hours do you usually get, Robert? On a weeknight, I mean.

Can I have something to eat?

Of course, I said. I cleared my throat—a habit of mine, and not the kind of habit I can easily ignore. What would you like?

I get a choice?

It's not a restaurant, Robert, but I've got a kitchen upstairs. I even bought a few items I thought you might like. I bought eggs. I never eat eggs myself.

I don't eat eggs. And don't call me Robert. It's Bob.

Everyone used to eat eggs, remember? Then I gave him a smile— big, toothy—but I don't think he saw me. He was looking down again, running a hand through his sparse hair. Obviously, despite my best efforts, he wasn't a happy man.

What about some oatmeal? he asked—still looking down.

You got it, Bob. Maple syrup, brown sugar, cream, milk?

Nothing else. Just oatmeal.

No milk?

Nothing.

— —

Sandhurst, a small town fifty miles up the Hudson from New York City, didn't seem like a particularly dangerous place. Certainly not in comparison to Alphabet City, the neighborhood where I lived in Manhattan until my parents died and I came into a bit of money.

But until I had a gun in my pocket I'd never realized that danger was always lurking in the shadows, toying with my imagination, screwing it up. I'm somewhat ashamed to say it, but the gun loosened my imagination. After those evening strolls through the neighborhood, I wrote most productively, even fluidly—no small feat in the meager world of my psychology. Yes, for once I wrote feverishly. Sentences came out of me like stray bullets.

What is a gun, after all? It's like an umbrella on a cloudy day. You tend to look *up* less. And so my mind had the luxury of wandering. Like a zone outside myself, it entertained wild notions—including ideas for putting the gun to some higher purpose.

— —

You can scream, you can holler, I said, but no one will hear you. I've soundproofed the basement. Twice. Sound won't travel up, down, right or left. Sound doesn't travel. It gets to the wall or ceiling and stops right there.

You're very proud of this, Bob said.

Do you have any idea just how difficult it is to soundproof a basement?

Personally, I haven't had cause to find out.

Well, it's not easy, I said—and I began to pace along my side of the chain-link fence. I was feeling a little proud to be finally sharing my secret accomplishment, even if Robert Partnow wasn't the ideal audience. He was still in his mood of recalcitrance, defiance, or what at times I took to be feigned indifference. The Porta-Potty is brand-new, I said—pointing to the polyethylene booth in the back without breaking stride. Use it at your whim.

My whim?

I cleared my throat, once and then twice. Your cuffs, Bob, are made of indestructible plastic.

Bob nodded. What's your name? he asked me—and it seemed odd, right then, that he hadn't asked before.

Evan. Evan Ulmer.

And you obviously know mine.

A television, I said—pointing at the set on his side of the fence. You probably don't even watch television. So to your left is a small library of books. I've stocked it with titles that I thought you might enjoy. I can get more, of course. I don't know your tastes, Bob, but I've made a few educated guesses. I've spared you the self-help crap. You must be tired of it.

So you know—

I've centered, as best I could, on the theme of writers. Novels about novelists, I said. But no Roth, no Updike, no white boys gone gray and soft in the dick. A little David Leavitt and Ian McEwan to keep things contemporary. Have you read Joyce's *Portrait* lately?

No.

Staring at Bob, secretly worrying about my choices for this little library of his, I knew I was talking off the top of my head—babbling out of anxiety more than anything else. But then, what was the alternative?

Anyway, I said, I think you'll see you've got a pretty decent deal here. The refrigerator is small but sufficient, I hope. I have zero interest in harming you or making your life uncomfortable during your confinement, if that makes any sense.

It makes little sense, Bob said.

I mean no harm. And there's obviously no question of a ransom.

I don't understand.

I hope in time you will, I said—nodding, and in that moment I was hoping this for myself as well.

In fact, with Bob as my guest, I was doing a lot of hoping—wishing of the sort that makes you speak in an officious tone. Still getting to know my captive—*my editor,* I almost said—I was acting as though I knew what I was doing when, honestly, I didn't. And even if it was a little hard to listen to my own voice, I was determined. I was *not* going to screw this up.

A treadmill, I said—pointing to the brand-new apparatus. And it's a good one. Maybe a little short of what you'd find in your health club. Do you belong to a health club?

No.

I didn't think so. Mostly the treadmill's for walking, but it's entirely possible to jog, even with handcuffs.

What's the point of this? he said—closing his eyes, shaking his head.

You can do whatever you want, I said. But a word of advice. Coming from me, I know, any advice is suspect. But you might use this time, and your solitude, as an opportunity for reflection and physical exercise. And reading, of course. The television is here for your entertainment, Bob. But it's the only one in the house and so we'll have to share it.

What is it that you want?

I used the word *solitude,* I said. Compared to your office environment, and probably your home life, you'll be living in a kind of solitude. And yet I'm here, too. I live in this house. Essentially we're roommates. I have the key, you have the television. I use the bathroom, you use the Porta-Potty. I live upstairs, you live downstairs, but I think we'll probably be spending some time together.

What exactly does *that* mean?

You're an intelligent man, I said. I'm an intelligent man. We have things to talk about.

— —

What exactly is a girlfriend?

My last girlfriend hadn't really been one, not in the strictest sense. We hadn't gotten around to sleeping together, and obviously—the way things fizzled, petered out—the whole question of fidelity hadn't risen to the point of discussion. The last time I saw her, in my apartment on Houston Street, she'd told me she was going on a blind date that coming Friday. And so she couldn't have dinner with me—not on that particular night. Maybe another night would work.

I'd carefully considered how to respond, and I was trying to align my response with whatever it was she wanted—whether she knew what she wanted or not. And what did she want? Did she want me to be accommodating? Did she want me to show I had enough confidence to wait it out? Did she want me to pull out my dick and draw a line in the sand? Was I supposed to say to her, *Listen, you're making a mistake, honey. You've already hit the jackpot right here. That guy is just a waste of your time, and so why don't you skip the tedium of finding out that I'm the best thing that's ever happened to your little bitch ass?*

Not that I would ever have said that. Someone else, someone bolder—not me.

— —

Promise Buckley lived only a couple of blocks away, it turned out. Funny how I'd never seen her before in Sandhurst. And in a mere two months, I thought I'd seen *everyone*—for better or worse.

Right from the start I liked everything about her except her name.

— —

Robert Partnow, his face creased with a smile, sits behind a desk cluttered with paper, magazines, newspapers, and books. A pair of eyeglasses dangle from one hand—a show of vanity for a camera that demands it. Two columns of manuscripts in their boxes, slightly out of focus, sit precariously on the foregrounded corners of the desk. It's one of those simple but somewhat gaudy French antiques—thin top, no drawers, gold molding along the curvy edges. You expect its owner to be wearing a double-breasted suit, looking like some literary equivalent of Donald Trump. Robert Partnow is, instead, unpretentiously tieless in a long-sleeved knit shirt.

On a relatively warm day in late February, I'd found this picture, along with a short article, at the public library across the street from the Museum of Modern Art. (This was right before

I left Manhattan, my belongings already cloistered in the orange and white U-Haul.) The article described a minor reshuffling of the beleaguered editorial staff at what was "once one of the largest and most prestigious publishing houses in New York." Although it had been recently downsized, stripped of a significant paperback imprint, the house was still very much afloat—or so Mr. Partnow insisted. And even if books in the self-help genre were now a more dominant part of the list, the strengths of the house still lay in the quality of its fiction and nonfiction.

That picture, torn from the magazine and folded twice, found its way into the interior pocket of my long gabardine coat.

——

Right from the start I liked everything about her except her name. I thought a lot about names, chose them carefully when I had the authorial privilege. I kept a list of possibilities. And Promise was the kind of name—Candy, Hope, Summer, Tuesday—that you could never quite get past. Because of its overtness, it was not a name that really appealed to me.

Promise had recently returned from a trip to Prague, a kind of belated graduation gift from her parents. Now she was living temporarily in her parents' house in Sandhurst—their weekend getaway for most of her childhood.

If Promise wasn't quite pretty, she wasn't plain, either. She had a round face, its surface slightly rough and porous, beautiful lips, and a perfect nose—larger than necessary, some might think. Tall, she had brunette hair that hung straight and grazed her shoulders. (*Hair without a blueprint,* she later called it.) I especially liked her eyes, which were big and blue and guileless. For me this was an achievement—avoiding guile, feeling *not* drawn to it, or feeling drawn along by something else.

I met her at the Sandhurst Public Library, which barely passed for a library. The librarians were dawdling, charmless, and slow-witted. They hadn't shelved any titles published within the past six months. The restrooms were surprisingly dirty. Somehow the Sandhurst Public Library wasn't really a systematic enterprise. Still, I felt calm there, which had always been the effect libraries had on me, since boyhood; and I became a regular after Bob entered my life. It felt like a good idea to escape the house occasionally and leave him to his own devices, if only because it reminded me that *I* wasn't the prisoner.

Promise and I were both in the A-G fiction aisle one day, and then the next day we found ourselves in that same aisle again.

— ◼ —

That picture, torn from the magazine and folded twice, found its way into the interior pocket of my long gabardine coat. Standing in Midtown the day after a freaky April snowstorm that nearly nixed my plans, I unfolded the picture and stared at the man I was about to meet. Despite the thinning hair at the front of his head and the goofy smile, Robert Partnow wasn't such a bad-looking fellow. Slightly overweight, maybe. He was like a dark-haired cross between John Malkovich and Kelsey Grammer. He looked nice, even charming—not particularly studious or bookish, which was how I'd imagined him when I came across his name.

Pausing at the southwest corner of Madison and Forty-eighth, I surveyed the other three corners of the intersection. The snow was already becoming a muddy, sludgy mess—too many cars, too many people. What was I looking for? Mostly I was looking for someone looking for me. Normally you walk through life with a narcissistic audience of one; now I had the disturbing feeling that *everyone* was watching me. As you might imagine, it was a rush—but it was also disconcerting. And at that moment I was glad I'd decided against wearing a hat, which might've attracted more attention. In a white shirt, a long coat, and a pair of blue jeans, I felt relatively anonymous.

Stopping in front of the Evergreen Building, I looked back toward the street and saw nothing but the usual bustle—the back-and-forth haste of sidewalk traffic at one-thirty in the afternoon. Inside the building I found a lobby roughly the size of my childhood home in Wisconsin, with eight elevators arranged in two sets of four. A young African American woman in a blue outfit sat at a security station, behind a wooden counter with a bold, undulating design. What was she doing? As she looked down at something in front of her—a magazine, her nails, a log of last night's visitors—people walked by without glancing in her direction.

I knew I couldn't afford to be recorded in her memory, loitering in the lobby and looking aimless, a small bulge in the pocket of my coat. So I went outside again and stood near the entrance to the building. Spotting a man walking past with a Seeing-Eye dog, I considered myself lucky—for once.

And then I saw him, Robert Partnow, walking toward me, hidden among the masses—or almost.

— —

Promise and I were both in the A-G fiction aisle one day, and then the next day we found ourselves in that same aisle again. Two days after that, on the last day of April, it happened yet again—this time it was Promise in H-P, me in Q-V. We saw each other through the stacks, in between the shelves. She was far enough away for safety but close enough for comment. A mutual wave of acknowledgment passed between us, and then, at a closer distance, a whispered conversation about the trials of dealing with sloppy shelving and the muddle of Dewey decimals (which the library used for everything *but* fiction). She had a sympathetic way of rolling her eyes, I noticed—unusual, I thought, in a woman her age.

Promise was a decade and a half younger than me, and yet we had in common an interest in reading fiction and, more importantly, in becoming what she referred to as *professional writers*. I didn't particularly like that way of putting it; it made me think of someone who went to a job every day, churning out computer manuals or press releases or text for greeting cards. (Or proofreading for that matter—which was what I used to do, back in New York City, for too many years.) But I could see why Promise liked the aura of professionalism, why the designation appealed. Neat in appearance, she always kept at her library table a collection of mechanical pencils along with her trio of wire-bound journals and a copy of Kafka's diaries. Promise liked the workaday rubric of a vocation, even if her own ambitions were strictly literary. She'd recently tried to explain her activities in Sandhurst to her parents by drawing parallels to her father's law practice—an office, a schedule, meetings. Meetings that took place between her and herself, she told me.

Apparently, Promise believed in structure as much as she believed in herself.

— —

And then I saw him, Robert Partnow, walking toward me, hidden among the masses—or almost. And for once there wasn't any doubt in my mind—just the pull of inevitability, the gravity that keeps the snowball rolling. It was like a voice, egging me on. It was *my* voice, it seemed, uttering a name that had been floating in my head for days. And the man to whom I'd addressed this name, in the form of a question—he turned, stopped, looked at me and smiled.

Right then I realized the power of my own voice. It felt as though I'd spoken underwater, but apparently he'd heard me. And, bolstered, I went on to speak the words I'd learned by heart. *Right now, if you look down for a moment, you can see I'm holding a gun and it's pointed at you.* And with my hand deep in the pocket of my coat, I pointed the gun in his direction, even though I realized, right then and there, that it looked like it could've been anything—a finger, a screwdriver, a compact camera. It was not the most effective show of force. In the movies, where I must've gotten some of what I was doing, this maneuver seemed to carry more weight. *I'll pull the trigger if you move, scream, or try anything whatsoever, and if you understand what I'm saying, please nod.* The man's head bobbed.

Given the circumstances, he seemed remarkably coolheaded—

moving and reacting to my words with the poise of an actor remembering his lines. He'd stopped smiling, but he didn't show any
outward anxiety. He merely repositioned his leather satchel on his
shoulder and waited.

Do you want me to—

I want you to turn right on Lexington, and then I'll give you
further instructions. OK. Now please start walking.

What is this about?

It's about you, Mr. Partnow. And it's about me. Please now.

And together, following my instructions, we walked down the
sidewalk, choosing our steps in yesterday's melting snow, toward
Lexington. I made a threat or two along the way to impress upon
him my resolve, but it probably wasn't necessary. Robert Partnow
was docile. The ease with which I carried out my plan reminded
me—not right then and there, but later—of the time I stole a Three
Musketeers bar at Morton's Pharmacy and found out how oblivious
the world could be.

—•—

Apparently, Promise believed in structure as much as she believed
in herself. That was one reason why I liked her. She also endeared
herself to me by using inventive swear words to complain about
the library restrooms and the flickering fluorescent lights that
made "reading corner"—across the way from where we sat, at the
tables—a misnomer. If she didn't like order quite as much as I did
(my fastidiousness likely learned from years of proofreading), she
came very close. And her powers of organization—the tidy way
she kept her writing things—were just part of her overall zeal. She
wrote easily, without the self-consciousness that made writing such
a burden for me. Was this zeal the effect of her Yale education? I
steered clear of the irony with which I typically sized up others'
enthusiasms. She was only twenty-five years old, so why shouldn't
she exude hope at being a writer whose career would, in her chosen
field, rival her father's? And wasn't she smart to skip over the joke

of a graduate degree in creative writing, which had been my own particular method of wasting a year and a few thousand dollars?

If she'd gone further, entertained notions of grandeur, assumed she'd make as much money as her father, then I might've needed to intervene and set her straight. But Promise knew better. Unlike me, she'd grown up around the rudiments of culture—concerts, museums, galleries. She'd been given a charmed but worldly perspective on artists. Most of them didn't make a lot of money, and the others—like the ones she'd met at literary gatherings and the pre-Whitney Biennial parties her parents sometimes hosted—were the exceptions. These fortunate few who hit the jackpot, she told me, suggested only a serendipitous combination of talent and circumstance.

— —

I don't know, Bob said—shrugging, gently lifting his cuffed hands.

I was just wondering, I said—keeping my eyes on the television, trying hard to soft-pedal my inquiry into the logic of marital infidelity.

I mean, you think about asking someone out, he said. You think about sleeping with someone when you're not supposed to sleep with someone, when the consequences of sleeping with someone are enormous and dangerous. But you do it. You sleep with someone and it's wonderful and it makes life messy, and so what?

I can't believe you're saying this, I said—my eyes taking leave of Maury Povich and the chubby woman who claimed to have committed over two dozen acts of infidelity.

Why?

I don't really know you, Bob, but it just seems weird for you to be saying this. Are you speaking from personal experience?

I'm speaking theoretically.

Because if you're speaking from personal experience, it would help to know the particulars.

Particulars?

Because I'm interested in learning from you.

Learning from me, Bob said, slowly—trying the words on for size. Learning what? How do you mean? You mean, as if *my* life is in good shape?

Isn't it?

It's OK. A little messy, really, but—

Messy in what way? I asked.

There's a lot going on.

You're a busy man.

Yes, he said, I'm a busy man.

What are you busy with?

Everything.

I feel like you're avoiding me, Bob.

—•—

I like whispering, Promise said—doing just that, across the library table.

You do?

It makes words seem almost forbidden, don't you think?

She'd been sitting there by herself when I arrived. And I'd asked if it was OK to sit down at her table, not in words but by signaling with my finger—wagging it between me and the empty chair. Her response had been sufficient, if slightly disappointing; she'd nodded after shrugging her shoulders. Sitting down, I'd opened my brief-case and written for thirty minutes in silence; the only interruption so far had been an exchange of smiles. And so, considering that we hadn't been whispering, that our whispering had been initiated by her whispered question, I wasn't sure how to respond.

Where else do you whisper? I said. I mean, besides in libraries.

In theaters. In the presence of sleeping children. In church.

You attend a church?

No, my mother does, she said—rolling her eyes. And I go with her sometimes.

So you whisper to your mother?

Never, she said—as emphatically as she could in a whisper. Not to her.

I wanted to understand, to ask Promise a few more questions, but I found myself oddly exhausted from the whispering. It was, in fact, difficult work, whispering for any length of time, at least across a table in a public library. Or maybe it had nothing to do with whispering. Maybe it was simply the toil of conversing with a young woman I found intriguing. Could I keep up with her? Could I continue whispering without, willy-nilly, divulging too much?

I leaned back in my chair, smiled, and returned to my green notebook—my haven, my shell, my lifelong excuse for not quite living.

2

—◀o▶—

An avid reader as a child, and a watcher of television and the movies, I never managed to let go of that fantasy of being a character in a story—someone whose life is observed by an omniscient narrator, seen through the lens of a camera that feeds its audience even as it flatters its subject. I've always wanted to be seen, and to see myself, as an actor in the world. I've wanted my life to take shape—my every step, my every word. For beginners, could someone please look inside my green notebooks, where I write daily, or at least aspire to, cataloging thoughts and fantasies, doubts and elaborate scenarios of sweet retribution? It's here, when I'm not totally blocked, that my fiction gets generated—primordially, in an early sticky goo. My thoughts are crude, my prose is rough, but I'm alive. These pages are like thick plates of glass that I hold up and breathe on, over and over. And my fiction, it's a window on everything I want for myself but can't have.

How long have you worked in publishing? I asked—backtracking, trying a new tack. After five minutes of conversation, commenced after a dinner of pork chops and the nightly news, I was frustrated; my voice had arrived at a shrill, incredulous tone.

Twenty-two years, Bob said—and he sighed.

And so twenty-two years tells you the industry hasn't changed.

I didn't say that. You've got to be kidding, it's changed enormously. It's not a dishonorable profession, that's all I said.

Did I say it was *dishonorable?*

OK, no, you didn't use the word, but that's what you meant. You haven't been able to publish, and that makes you angry, and—

Blah, blah, blah. Did I say I was angry?

No, Bob said, you went out and kidnapped me for altruistic reasons.

I didn't *kidnap* you. Anyway, what does it prove?

That you aren't particularly fond of editors, he said—leaning back in his chair, the cloth napkin sliding off his lap and onto the floor. *Book* editors, at least.

You think I like magazine editors?

I thought you said—

Stories in *journals,* Bob. Small, inconsequential journals. A magazine is not a journal.

Well, it proves you don't like *me.* And, if I can pat myself on the back for a moment, authors usually do.

I don't know what it proves, I said—suddenly unhappy with myself, with my abbreviated and paltry publishing history, my having brought Robert Partnow here to serve as a makeshift conscience. And it didn't help that the pork chops hadn't gone over very well. Apparently Bob had a sensitive stomach, in addition to what seemed like recurrent headaches and a general sluggishness he claimed as reason to avoid beginning his workouts on the treadmill.

But also I meant it—I didn't know why I'd put Bob in this situation. I hadn't had the luxury, during these first days of attention to the details of detainment, to speculate on reasons behind my actions, behind what I called *the abduction scenario*. Was I trying to come upon some otherwise elusive truth, to overcome the obstacle to my own happiness? To see someone else suffer the fate of staying put, feeling stuck in *today* with no hope of *tomorrow*? To return the favor after so many letters of rejection?

In devising the plan—buying the gun, building the basement fortress, tracking the daily movements of Robert Partnow—I hadn't allowed myself to analyze my actions. I hadn't searched after motivational mainsprings any more than I would've stopped a burst of creative activity, a sustained effort in one of my green notebooks, to worry about its source. But now I was beginning to wonder. Had I been fooling myself in thinking of the abduction as a brave act? Was I instead just a fuckup predictably fucking up, pushing the envelope even farther in the direction of desperation? Was I merely following a path already mapped by countless others, the dregs of humanity who didn't know how to take *no* for an answer?

I wanted to learn something about the publishing industry, I finally said—and surely that was one of my motivations, if not the most salient.

Couldn't you have gone to the library? Bob said—lowering his chin, resting it on his couplet of cuffed hands, and looking at me over his glasses.

From the inside, I said. I wanted to learn from the inside.

Couldn't we have just gone out to lunch?

— ▪ —

My life? I said.

We were sitting in the Mealtime Cafe, a local joint—a Sandhurst institution, Promise claimed—complete with a creaky screen door that closed with a *thwack*. It was disconcerting at first, and then you got used to it, along with the smell of bacon in the middle of the afternoon. She'd invited me.

I'm not asking you to look into the future, she said. Just up until now. You know, your life so far.

These were the kinds of questions that made me pause and wonder again what had become of my solitude, my boredom, my loneliness. Three days after Bob had come into my life, I'd gone to the library and found, or finally had the opportunity to meet, Promise—a young woman who had no other friends in Sandhurst even though she seemed, if anything, friendly to a fault. Just who was Promise Buckley, and what might she do with an honest answer? To what degree did the situation call for half-truths, if only to slow down the inevitable baring of my soul?

It hasn't gone all that well, I said.

Was it fun being in graduate school in—

In Baltimore, I said. And no it wasn't.

But you haven't given up. You *are* writing.

A couple of novels, I said. Neither published. I just get tired from time to time.

To start with my mind, and heal that, would require the stamina of a furniture mover. That's Kafka, she said. From his diaries.

I nodded. I looked over as a mother and her two young children— boy and girl in matching red-stripe outfits—entered the restaurant. The mother couldn't have been a day older than Promise. *Thwack.*

I'm assuming, Promise said, that you're talking about your writing when you say things haven't gone that well. Maybe that's me being presumptuous.

No, that's you being kind, I said—and smiled the sort of smile that almost hurts, that sinks your soul. It was a smile my mother taught me.

Evan, have you ever been married?

—•—

Couldn't we have just gone out to lunch?

How was I to react to this ploy of Bob's—this retrospective chumminess that rendered the abduction scenario superfluous?

Bob, let's be honest. You'd never have agreed to have lunch with me.

Who says?

Bob, let's be honest. A kind of mantra that I'd gotten into the habit of uttering during these first several days, as though trust could be induced by twisting the arm of a detainee. I should've known better.

Maybe if I'd had a story in the latest *Harper's,* I said. Or was friends with Martin Amis. Or better yet his agent. Who *is* his agent?

It wouldn't have done you any good, Bob said—sighing. The story in *Harper's.* Maybe once, in the old days.

What about the agent?

You've got to remember, Evan, I've been at this awhile. My curiosity has waned along the way. I'm not as hungry as I used to be. Maybe you kidnapped the wrong guy.

Book publishing is fluid is what I hear, I said—making a fluttering motion with my hand. I read about it in *Publishers Weekly.* Nothing's established, like in those old days you were talking about. Profit is everything. The days of slapdash P&L statements are over.

Well, I'm not sure those days—

And that makes for nervous editors. And nervous editors tend to be flighty.

You read *Publishers Weekly?*

I'm a subscriber, I said.

Bob slowly shook his head. Its listless, back-and-forth movement made me feel almost pitiful. Did he know this? Was that why he did it?

What if I talk for sixteen hours, he said, and tell you everything I know about the industry? I'll tell you about the old days. The majesty of Knopf, the legacy of Bennett Cerf. I'll tell you about Bertelsmann and the earlier takeovers you don't hear so much about. You know, the bloodletting and those of us who survived and how we did it.

That whole fiasco over at Random House a couple of years ago. You'll get it straight from the horse's mouth. You'll write it down, and together we'll consider the implications for you. For your career. If I did that, then—

That's not really it, I said—and I could feel my forehead going taut. Clearing my throat, I tried to summon whatever *it* was. But what was it? Something beyond me—a whisper hidden inside a wooden box with a heavy, heavy lock. The voice of truth in the ear of the deaf. *It* was what I wanted to get rid of in the worst way—I knew that much. Whatever was driving me to small acts of malice needed to be let loose.

— —

In the first month I lived in Sandhurst, I'd gone down to the basement of my house exactly once—to stow skis, a bicycle, boxes of memorabilia. Apparently the previous owners of the house had used the basement as a den. You could see the deep indentations in the shag carpet where the pool table had once stood. An old dartboard, covered in spiderwebs and without a dart in sight, still hung on one wood-paneled wall.

My first order of business was to tidy up the electrical wiring; it was running wildly along the rafters of the ceiling. I installed two layers of soundproofing—150 mm acoustic rolls, deep chocolate brown in color—that covered the rafters, and then did the same for the walls of the basement. I ripped up the shag carpeting. In a compromise of plumbing, I rigged up a pipe from a washer/dryer hookup at the base of the stairs to a Porta-Potty purchased with cash in the Lower East Side. I put a new faucet on the large basin. I bought heavy chain-link fencing that came in rolls of thirty-six feet and then experimented with the concrete and cinder blocks that would eventually anchor the fence and prevent what in my mind I called *the under-the-fence escape scenario*. It took me a day and a half just to create the hinge assembly on the rectangular food slot in the fence, just under the lock apparatus.

Everything seemed difficult, then easy, then difficult again. A little too late in the game, I bought a copy of *Finishing Basements and Attics: Ideas and Projects for Expanding Your Living Space*. Mixing cement, it turned out, was like mixing oatmeal; but as soon as you stopped mixing it, it became dry and unmanageable and useless. I found this out by trial and error—there was no easy way to get advice at the local hardware store about how best to build a fortress in your basement.

The process was anything but intuitive. I could see why talking heads spoke of *the trail of evidence:* bomb manuals downloaded from the Internet or books on military demolitions checked out of the library by some loser with a grudge. A Mafia fledgling or terrorist recruit could query someone in the family; for the rest of us— the so-called lonely fucks of the world—it was pretty much touch and go.

I knew one thing. My venture required a mind that could work logically within its own empty corridors. *Keep your eye on the ball,* my father would've said. And it was best to eschew any financial aspirations. Obviously, expecting a payoff would be hubris; and in that sense, the day-to-day life of an abduction artist wasn't so different from that of an aspiring novelist.

— -

They'd trace the call, I said.

OK, right, Bob said. I wasn't thinking. But what about a little note? I'll just write a few words saying I'm OK. You can read the note, and then we'll put it in the mail. Or *you'll* put it in the mail, obviously. And you can't mail it from here, I know, but—

I could go to New York and put it in the mail.

Exactly. And my wife Claudia gets the letter and knows I'm OK. I'm not dead.

And what exactly would this letter say?

I'm doing fine, he said, *I'm alive and healthy.*

What else? *Wish you were here?*

Bob closed his eyes, then opened them and gave me a withering look—the look he reserved, I imagined, for his wife in her worst moments.

I don't know, I said—shaking my head. Wouldn't it sound like you just took off on a vacation?

That might be good.

No, not good, Bob. Bad for your image. Suntanning somewhere in the Mediterranean, girls all around you. And not very believable.

We could mention—

The abduction? I said. I don't think so. By the way, Bob, do you mind slipping any dirty clothes through the slot? Tomorrow's Wednesday. Laundry day, as I think I told you.

— · —

Evan, have you ever been married?

No.

It was the truth, of course, and that counted for something—to me, if not to Promise. And in the moment it felt better to be answering in the negative. There's a certain time in anyone's life, isn't there, when *no* suggests an absence of baggage? It suggests a simpler sort of failure, with fewer casualties scattered along the road. Just me and my crown of thorns. It's never exactly the truth, things being far from simple; but it's the impression given by those, me included, who are considerate enough to hold off the spillage of details. If nothing else, I was polite—especially in the company of women.

My mother, from whom I learned politeness, used to say—in my presence, to the curious among her relatives and friends—that I just hadn't found the right girl yet. She always said *yet*—relying, as I see it now, on the word's subtle mixture of hope and onus.

In the booth at the Mealtime Cafe, Promise began to say something about a wedding she'd recently attended—but then the waitress showed up, two plates doing their balancing trick on her outstretched arm. I leaned back as Promise and I were served our greasy lunches on huge white plates with oversize pickles—like meals in themselves. Picking up my pickle, I imagined how all of this might be different if

I were more successful—if I'd published a book or two, let's say. I'd be offering my time to an impressionable beginner, and she'd be mooning over my accomplishments, my prestige, my wisdom. And—the way these things work, for better or worse—she'd be imagining my gentle hands on her buttocks as she rocked eagerly toward another climax.

What's going through your head? Promise said—her lips jutting, a quizzical look on her face, her eyebrows screwed up in a lovely way.

—　—

Six days? Really? I wasn't counting.

They said five on television, Bob said, but it's been six.

Maybe they aren't counting the day of the abduction, I said—sitting back in my chair, my feet braced against the fence. I held my hands in front of me, fingers spread. I stared at them, and then looked beyond them at the television. The sound was off, and Peter Jennings was moving his mouth and occasionally, abruptly, bobbing his head. Without the benefit of the auditory element, he looked like someone's spastic brother.

Well, I feel bad, I said. I feel bad about it in all sorts of ways.

What ways?

I wish I'd built that shower, I said—referring to our discussion the day before about Bob's dislike of *sponge baths,* as he called them. (He was proving more fastidious than I would've guessed; with a washcloth dipped into the large basin filled with soapy water, Bob washed his body and let it air-dry, but never with much satisfaction.) But I'm really not feeling very regretful, I said. I set out to do something, and guess what? You're here, Bob. I did it. And it wasn't easy. Maybe it *looked* easy—

To who?

To *whom,* I said. But it wasn't. It wasn't easy at all.

Why is it necessary that this comes at my expense? Bob asked—

switching off the television with the remote. Sam Donaldson—
standing in front of the steps to Congress, his old haunt—warped
and then disappeared, and Bob turned his full attention to me.
Couldn't you have built a ham radio or run in a marathon? And why
does it have to be done *to* anyone? Do you have to inflict harm on
someone to have your little feeling of success?

My *little* feeling of success?

Your success. Your—

My *feeling* of success, I said—standing up.

Do you want me to apologize?

No, I said—moving toward the stairs that led to the main floor
of the house. Speak your mind, Bob. That's what this is all about.
But it's coming up on seven o'clock and I'm not in the mood to
cook. And what am I supposed to do about *that*?

— ▪ —

Once in Sandhurst—my gear unloaded, my days of proofreading
mercifully behind me—I think I was hoping to find someone to
relieve my loneliness. (Don't believe what they say: it's more interesting being lonely in the big city than in the boondocks.) I thought
about Bob that way even before I'd met him, on the strength of
that one picture excised from the pages of *Publishers Weekly*. And
once he was set up in the basement, I couldn't help believing that in
different circumstances—in some other, simpler world—we might
be pals, Bob and me. In this spirit, sitting in my bedroom or at the
kitchen table or driving to the library, I sometimes spun fantasies
that we'd *both* been abducted. We were stuck with each other. (I
even thought about writing about it—a kind of updated *Robinson
Crusoe*.) Together we sat in our chain-link cell, getting to know each
other. We complained about our lousy treatment, examined the
strange circumstances of our confinement. I sympathized when
Bob got one of his migraine headaches, or when his sensitive in-
nards sent him sprinting to the Porta-Potty. And even if, back in real

life—in the normal course of things—we would never have become friends, we *did* become friends. Friends for life, like seatmates from strikingly different backgrounds who survive a plane crash.

Bob and I shared something—or so went this little story in my head. And more importantly we'd developed an implicit partnership. Thrown together, editor and author, both of us victims of captivity and an excess of television, we couldn't help but create our own cynical language of love and despair. We kept track of the daily news of our abduction, seen from afar. We became understandably jaded. We found ourselves smirking at the women who broke down on Sally Jessy Raphael over the heartache of a husband lost to Alzheimer's. We rated the news anchors according to consistency of hairstyle. We speculated on the sexual preferences of Katie Couric—a fellator, we both agreed.

— —

What's going through your head? Promise said—her lips jutting, a quizzical look on her face, her eyebrows screwed up in a lovely way.

Why?

You looked—

What. I looked what?

For a moment there you looked a little lost.

Lost? Me? Clearing my throat, I smiled at Promise.

Isn't it weird? she said.

What?

Getting lost. The idea of it. How it's a bad thing, because you can't find the street or whatever. And then it's a good thing, it's a way of saying that time is passing and who the fuck cares. It's like that song, "Let's Get Lost." You know that song?

Chet Baker.

For me, it's Susannah McCorkle. My parents own that CD. Anyway, good things are happening and you don't know why and you don't care. And there's no better way of saying what it feels like when things are going well.

Are we talking about writing?

We're talking about *everything,* Promise said.

— —

It rained the entire day Wednesday, and I hate rain, but I didn't even care. At Larry's Hardware, I bought lightbulbs and a set of AA batteries. At the Bakery Village, the young woman behind the counter filled a pink box with doughnuts, bound the box with string, and then broke off the thread with her teeth. At Bubbles Coin Laundry, I got quarters and washed clothes and bedding and a pair of muddied sneakers. I felt the satisfaction of interacting with others and ticking items off a list of things that demanded attention.

A facile satisfaction, maybe, but it was like a shot of adrenaline after days of being cooped up. Was this a revelation about small-town living, that it only made sense as an escape from domestic confinement? (In New York, the assaults always came from the outside.) I had my trips to the library, of course, but somehow those seemed like another form of insularity.

The everyday chores of this day left me almost giddy. It was an odd sensation, as if I'd been released from my own abduction. I wasn't so much Evan Ulmer as Robert Partnow—delivered from captivity and choosing to spend a few hours in Sandhurst, making the rounds, wearing someone else's clothes, and acting like a local before submitting to the ordeal of calling the authorities and announcing his return to the real world.

Later, with the laundry bundled and still warm, and the box of doughnuts in the backseat, I decided to drive home the long way— down Swenson Street, past the house that Promise had described as her own. I didn't really have the address. As I got closer, I worried that I wouldn't be able to pick it out. But then I saw it, through the waving of windshield wipers—not the house itself, but the purple-and-green mailbox in the shape of an alligator's snout, next to the driveway. She'd described it to me one day at the library—it had been a childhood request, her parents acquiescing—but until that moment I'd forgotten all about it.

— —

What's it about?

It's going nowhere, I said.

OK. But what's it about? Is it in there? Bob asked—pointing with his chin to the brown leather briefcase hanging from my one hand.

In my other hand was a plastic bag of Chinese takeout. Bob was lying on the top bunk, propped on one elbow, looking almost carefree during this, his seventh day of captivity; through my sunglasses—which I was still wearing, having just returned from the library by way of Canton Express—I saw him as a peer, a roomie, a colleague in distress.

It's about unrequited love, I said—thinking back, trying to remember.

There's a good topic. A universal. Is it about a writer?

A writer? No. It's about a man who gives up on one woman and looks for another. I've only got two chapters. I don't know, I'm very unsure about the whole thing. I'm still searching for a plot.

Can I see? he said.

See?

Bob nodded, his eyes on the briefcase.

No.

Why not?

Why would you want to see it anyway?

I'm bored, Bob said—looking about the basement as though his confinement might explain the urge. And it's sort of what I do for a living.

You miss it?

Not exactly, he said. Read me a passage, Evan.

Aren't you hungry? I asked—jiggling the bag with the food, a substance I knew to be high on the list of desired objects in Bob's life, or at least in comparison to the drivel of my restless mind.

Read first, he said. Read me a passage.

I stared at Bob. *Read me a passage, read me a passage*—the words reverberating in my head. How long had it been since I'd read something aloud to someone other than myself? How long since I'd taken on my own voice, my fictional voice?

As a favor, Bob said—his cuffed hands clasped, looking intercessional.

I can't explain why, but I did it. I'd had a good day of writing and Promise and I had chatted for longer than was appropriate on the steps to the library. Bob had done his hour on the treadmill, even jogging a bit (or so he said). I felt *up*. And so I stooped down, let go of the Chinese food, removed my sunglasses, and opened the briefcase on my knees. I didn't take out my current notebook—in which I'd been jotting quasifictional impressions of Bob and his predicament—but one from years before, to which I sometimes referred in moments of nostalgia.

All right, you get one page, I said—as though he might really care, as though supply wasn't up to demand.

I cracked open the notebook, as Bob lay back on his bed.

Is it fun to be beautiful? I read the words aloud. *She'd been naked lying there in the bed, and then a minute later she was sitting up in blue jeans and a white shirt that could've been his. The shirt spoke to him of things simple. Undefiled. A stain, however small, would have ruined everything. And he was wondering what it felt like to add to your beautiful self the simple flourish of a crisp, freshly laundered white shirt. How the one means nothing or not as much without the other, nothing being quite good enough without its complement. A good, simple feeling is how he imagined it. Coming in from the cold, the bitter cold, and jumping into a hot bath. Having your sins forgiven for no good reason. Standing out in the middle of nowhere and having a long piss against the base of an innocent tree. It was the feeling of being relieved of something without having to go to any special trouble. That's what he'd meant by fun. She hadn't understood. She'd taken the question the wrong way, assumed he was saying something about her life and how facile it was. She considered her life far from easy. She was wrong about that, but that was beside the point.*

When I looked up from the page, Bob had his eyes closed.

Have I put you to sleep?

Not at all, he said—opening them.

You asked.

I did ask, he said. And thanks. It reminds me of—

Listen, I said—shutting my briefcase and reaching for the bag of Chinese takeout. I know you liked those sweet and sour spareribs. But I thought prawns with snow peas might be a better choice. You know, all things considered.

3

I desperately wanted to succeed. Or, more accurately, I wanted to succeed at being a writer, which wasn't the career my father wanted for me. If I'd become a lawyer or a dentist or even a schoolteacher, he would've been happy, I think. Actually, happy *isn't quite the right word, since my father wasn't really a happy person. But he would've been pleased with my career choice. He would've nodded his head slowly and smiled reluctantly, which was his way of jumping up and down and screaming for joy.*

Becoming a newspaperman might have made a little sense to him, but a writer of fiction? My father was not, himself, a reader. He was a doer. By profession a speculator in real estate, an investor in retirement communities—old-age bunkers, he called them, before he became old enough to enter one himself. His sleeves rolled up and stern resolve etched on his face (I've always had my mother's face, round and soft), my father provided for his family. He even got lucky at the end, which was lucky for me—he enabled my move to Sandhurst and this modest house and the freedom to pursue my writing. He couldn't have intended this, any more than I ever meant to use my freedom to take away another's.

My father died first, from a heart attack; and then, a year and a half later, my mother dissolved in a matter of weeks from lung cancer. I don't blame them for dying like that, and in many ways it was an undisguised blessing—the swiftness. They were here, *then they were* there. *(It was my mother, the impatient one, who taught me to pull Band-Aids off quickly, without thinking.) Without any siblings, I was left more or less alone in the world, but it could've been worse; and for the first couple of months—back in New York, resorting to the air conditioner that awful summer, telling this and that law firm that, thanks but no, I'm no longer proofreading—there was a feeling of freedom, a sense that their deaths, and particularly my father's, allowed me some latitude.*

The monkey was off my back, so to speak. Or so I thought.

M Y ALMOST DAILY CONVERSATIONS with Promise left me
dazed and giddy. Speaking to her at the library, in the park,
or on the phone—it felt like rolling dice, like busting through an
unmarked door, like losing your balance on the edge of your very
own roof. You were never quite sure what was going to happen
next, where you might land. This wasn't a new feeling, I realized,
though in the past it always had to do with fantasy rather than
reality—with wishes that went astray or incorporated bits of incon-
gruent, so-called reality. Reality itself, the real item—the day-to-day
movements of life, or at least the life that had been mine—seemed
predetermined by comparison. Real conversations followed the
script. It was only in fantasies, it seemed, that I could scare myself.

Now, with Promise, something had changed. For once, real life
had become somewhat fantastical. It was like watching a movie,
reading a book, having a dream. I was waiting to find out what
would happen next. Reality was impinging on my imagination,
knocking insistently on the door. I kept wanting to turn the page,
to go faster—either that or shut my eyes and let things progress by
way of reverie. Sometimes, at the library, it felt like I might as well
have had my pajamas on, my eyes closed, a pillow under my weight-
less head.

Did I deserve this? Did I deserve *her*?

— —

When he was standing, Bob often clenched his fingers, I noticed.
Maybe it was easier on his wrists. From my point of view, he had
the look of a man on the edge of drawing a gun from beneath his
waistband—like Gary Cooper freeze-framed just before his fate
was to be determined. Bob complained about the handcuffs, but
to me they were a non-negotiable precaution. I gave in on the little

things—raspberries and Chap Stick and *un*scented toilet paper, and occasionally ice cream instead of frozen yogurt—but I had my limits. And, as I liked to remind him, I wasn't stupid.

One evening, just to see what it felt like, I tried on a pair of handcuffs, slightly larger than Bob's. I'd bought two pairs way back when, on the off chance that my captive's ankles might need securing as well as his hands. Now, wearing those cuffs, I found that fitting my hands together, fingers interlaced as if in prayer, allowed my wrists a little more comfort. (The gesture made me feel weak, of course, like it would any ex-believer.) I put the key on the floor at my feet.

Why are you doing that? he asked.

The handcuffs? I said. Just to make sure you're not going crazy.

Crazy? Don't you think *you're* the one who's crazy?

OK, Bob. Yes. Good point. But you come this far and you realize that craziness, that's just part of the game. You know, the anxiety over what it looks like or what it means or how it happened or what your mother would think. Whatever. It comes with the territory.

Bob nodded, taking on a tired expression. He looked almost weary, and I wondered what he was thinking. Was he now, already, exhausted by his keeper? Was he thinking of his own mother, living a lonely life up in Maine? Was he wondering whether the key, just a few feet away, fit both sets of handcuffs?

You think I'm crazy? I asked.

I think you're basically a good person. But—

What is a good person, Bob? And why would anyone want to be one? Are you? Are you a good person?

No, not really.

Why not?

I can be duplicitous.

Meaning—

I have flashes of goodness, he said, but—

And what makes me a good person?

Did I say—

Yes, you said I was a good person.

I don't know, Bob said. Maybe—

Keeping you here, in this cage?

I appreciate the Port-o-Johnnie.

Actually, it's called a Porta-Potty.

It's my only real privacy, he said. What did those poor guys in Iran do? Remember that?

I was a kid.

They must've just peed in their pants, over and over.

No, I said—sighing. I'm not the terrorist type. No, it's just me, Evan Ulmer, the master of envy. And the envious are often kind. Suspiciously so, wouldn't you say?

We both looked over at the half-size refrigerator when it turned on—its hum suddenly the only voice in the basement. It needed restocking, I realized. Yogurt, low-fat cottage cheese, pitted olives, bottled water, but *not* of the bubbly sort. According to Bob, anything carbonated was hard on his gut.

These things *do* hurt, I said—red marks already forming on my wrists, no matter how I held my hands.

Who do you envy, Evan?

Whom, I said.

Do you envy me?

No. No offense, but no.

Then who?

I envy the other guy, I said. The one named Evan Ulmer, the one who caught a break or the one who managed to kick aside a small little piece of dust in his imagination and write something that floored an agent, an editor. That's the one I envy. *Motherfucker.*

— ▬

And what did anger feel like? It felt like something mounting in my mind, gaining size and substance with each passing day. Or sometimes it was more of a wrenching in my chest—a twisting and turning, like a rubber band wrapped repeatedly around a finger, digging into the flesh. I felt it as a faint tremor, an early warning, the kind my father experienced, so I was told, a few days before his first heart attack. That's what anger could do to you, I decided. I imagined what it would feel like—writhing on the ground, unable to reach the telephone.

Was I angry at myself? Yes, maybe. Sometimes it came on very suddenly. I'd have temper tantrums over inconsequential things—a glass dropped, a button falling from a shirt, a wanton stream of urine bouncing off the rim of the toilet. These were *my* mistakes. But mostly, my anger, the tremor inside—it happened as a slow accretion, like everything else in my life. More the inhalation of an accordion, say, than the striking of a gong. And gradually it began to express itself outwardly, perhaps in tribute to my father, whose accusatory finger was almost always aiming *thataway*.

Oddly—or maybe not so oddly—I was most aware of this anger in California, while taking care of my mother when she was dying from cancer.

— —

OK, so here's what it is, Promise said—suddenly breathless. Sooner or later you realize it's entirely up to you. For all intents and purposes there's no one else. It's just you and this awful, tediously fucking task of reassuring yourself. And so if you're lucky, you've got this little person sitting up on your shoulder whispering words of encouragement.

She reached out and touched me—it was, I noted, the first time it had happened. We were standing in the sand, in the park a couple of blocks from the library, near the empty swings—a childless universe with the sun disappearing, evening approaching. She pressed down on my shoulder with her hand, and I dutifully lowered it as though it was weighted with the little person.

And that little man—

It's a man? I said—just as she withdrew her hand, returned it to its usual home at her side.

For the sake of argument, Promise said. Yes. And the little man is saying, *You can do it!* or *It's a piece of cake!* or *You just keep getting better and better, you rascal!*

Where do I get one of these little guys? I said—reaching across my chest and touching my shoulder, now suddenly bereft of hand, of little man.

What I'm wondering, Evan, is if this is how it works. Maybe you have to believe in yourself to get anywhere. And probably this is obvious, but it's sort of a revelation to me, the way it works backwards. The way you can't do anything without believing in yourself, and that's when it's hard to believe in yourself, if you haven't done anything. Which makes me think that maybe you can't really believe in yourself without deluding yourself.

Deluding yourself?

Just a little, she said—using her thumb and forefinger to show the size of the delusion, which seemed roughly, perhaps not coincidentally, the size of the little man as I'd been imagining him.

By living in a fantasy world? I said—looking down and twisting my foot in the sand to erase a line I'd drawn earlier, absentmindedly.

If that's what you want to call it, Promise said. Yes. A fantasy world. I'm not *telling* you so much as *asking*. And I'm not asking you so much as asking myself. I'm just wondering if that's how it works, if that's what it takes. That's all. You think I'm crazy?

— —

Did I deserve this? Did I deserve *her*? Had I in any way earned this woman's generosity of spirit? What, after all, did Promise and I have in common?

Strangely, we both did have a look—a conventional appearance, in both wardrobe and countenance, that allowed us to slip into anonymity, to skirt past the authorities (or whomever you skirt past these days). Promise wasn't dowdy in any sense—no plaid skirts, no thick glasses over anxious eyebrows—but there was a plainness to her, in her clothing and in her body and face. She had the kind of straight and even hair that danced predictably whenever she so much as thought of turning her head. I suppose she could've done something with it. She could've cut it off entirely or grown it very, very long. But with Promise there was a lot of middle ground—a vast, vacant lot of what seemed like normality—where a person like me could get lost.

Yes, she was more gregarious, less anxious than I was, less a loner and more a person only temporarily isolating herself for the benefit of her writing—her *art*. She had the distinction of being young. But getting to know Promise had been a process of opening myself to the surprise of who she was, who she *really* was—and she was someone other than the image she projected. We had that in common, too. After all, if you met me at a dinner party—the sort-of-quiet guy at the end of the table with impeccable table manners—you'd never guess that I could construct an abduction plan, let alone execute one.

— —

Oddly—or maybe not so oddly—I was most aware of this anger in California, while taking care of my mother when she was dying from cancer. I'd left New York and stayed for a month in Woodland Hills, outside of Los Angeles; she'd moved there to be near her sister after my father died.

Several things about my mother annoyed me—her impatience, the way she kept to herself, ignored my father (even though this showed her good sense), and eventually gave up on doing much of anything but sitting in her chair, smoking, reading her detective novels. As a child born to a mother in her mid-forties, I'd been an afterthought—more of a mistake than a surprise. By the time I was a teenager, and more so in my twenties, she was an indulgent sad sack—a quitter of everything but her cigarettes. And so old and tired, it seemed to me.

But there's a difference between being annoyed and being angry, and staying with her in that last month told me that I was lacking more than sympathy. Anger, I knew, was an inappropriate response to a dying parent. She was my mother, after all—the one who'd brought me into the world, albeit reluctantly. And what did she ask of me? She demanded nothing beyond her daily sandwiches, shorn of crusts and cut on the diagonal and slathered with mayonnaise. And she requested her son's hand to hold in moments of acute pain.

Eventually this anger—at my mother, and in defiance of my dead father—took on a more purposeful cast, at least within my imagination. My mind was spinning with schemes. Maybe it was the wanton atmosphere of California. Maybe it was television—its pleas, its infomercials and religious programming, its mixture of glut and vacuity. (I watched a lot of television late at night after my mother retired to her smoking den.) Or maybe it was my mother coughing up more and more blood on the bedsheets, and me conversing daily, and redundantly, with the posse of doctors.

In any case, my world suddenly seemed to hold a series of opportunities—from throwing a shoe at the television, to snapping the neck of the neighbor's yapping dog, to gagging my mother, shoving a sandwich down the hole that had sucked in the cigarette smoke in the first place. Or, for that matter, the thought came to me, what about abducting an editor at a major publishing house, keeping him in my own private Bastille, and delivering daily judgments like cool rejection slipped beneath a door nailed shut?

Everyone needs a little of their own medicine. Those words—they were bouncing off the walls of my mind, leaving me whirling with fantasies of bleak diagnoses and the invasive correctives I suddenly felt capable of.

Spending too much time with your mother, for the last time, can do that to you. Especially when you want a suitable ending—whatever the fuck that means, however it is that you're supposed to wave good-bye with the same hand out of which she's taken a few bites.

And so I concocted a plan to deal with the dog.

—•—

I allow you to go without the awful handcuffs, and the next day what do you do? You lie to me about Lloyd.

No, I didn't.

You told me he was a friend.

And anyway, so what? Bob said. What if I *did* lie?

I haven't lied to you. I've been—

Yes, of course, the epitome of moral righteousness. I know, I know.

I began to say something in response but stopped short. I thought better of engaging in a fruitless argument. More than a week had passed, and I was still trying to set a proper tone, encourage honesty, avoid unnecessary squabbles. We'd had our good moments, but a whiff of anger still lingered. I wanted to rid the basement of it, allow it its passage *out*—release it like some noxious gas.

I've been straight with you, I said.

So we're just skipping over the kidnapping, the abduction, whatever it is you call it.

I'm just wondering why you feel the need to lie.

You write fiction, Evan. Figure it out, take a wild guess.

I don't know what that means.

Writers make up shit, don't they? Bob said. And I just made up shit. I didn't write it down on a piece of paper, but—

When you write fiction, it comes in a package, I said—shaping one with my hands. You know this, Bob. And on the outside the package says, *This is made up. Objects in real life are not as interesting as they might appear.*

Staring hard at my less-than-truthful captive, I wrote the words in the air with an imaginary pen and then cleared my throat.

You're being naïve, he said. I appreciate you giving me the key for the handcuffs, but—

How can I believe anything you say?

You can't, Bob said—feigning sadness. Unfortunately everything that comes out of my mouth is potentially bullshit.

I'm starting to get that feeling.

Good. Get that feeling.

Do you even have a wife?

Of course I have a wife, Bob said — his cadence slowing, his voice a lower register. You've seen her on television.

— • —

And so I concocted a plan to deal with the dog. They say, in forensic literature, that people often begin with animals and then move on to humans. It's called *climbing the ladder of malfeasance.* I didn't abduct the neighbor's little yapping chihuahua, and I didn't strangle it as I'd imagined, over and over. Instead, I kissed my mother's forehead, excused myself for a few minutes, closed the door to her bedroom, and walked down the hall and out through the sliding-glass door into the backyard. Trudging across the grass that I'd been meaning to cut for a week, I tossed a long and expensive piece of pork tenderloin laced with arsenic (tucked into the meat, as I'd seen Julia Child do with garlic on television that morning) over the wooden fence. That ended the barking.

It was also, you could say, the first step in my ascent toward larger prey.

— • —

Shoplifting, Promise said. And kissing.

They go together? I asked.

Both were dangerous, she said. Or at least they *sounded* dangerous. I never ever got caught shoplifting, and I shoplifted quite a lot.

You don't seem the type, I said — with the phone cradled against my shoulder, my eyes closed, trying to imagine. I saw a girl's hand, expensive lingerie squeezed inside a fist and then pushed into a leather purse. Deeply. Furtively.

This is when I was younger, she said.

You don't even seem like the type who even *once* shoplifted.

Maybe I'm not whom you think I am, Evan.

It's *who,* I said—because I couldn't stop myself.

And when I was a teenager, I found out about it. I discovered it. And it just seemed like the most wonderful, perfect thing.

Stealing?

Kissing, Promise said. You could get away with it so easily. A kiss, big deal. How serious could a kiss be? No messiness, no pregnancies, no need to expose your body, no need to be fiddling with a boy's.

Fiddling, I said—because I liked the word.

And so I ended up kissing every boy who wanted to kiss me.

As a rule?

Yes. You could say that. I didn't broadcast it as some kind of policy decision, but—

And there were many? I asked.

I was *not* a looker, Promise said, especially not then, in high school. But I passed for cute on certain days. And remember, I was editor of the newspaper, and a homecoming princess. I had some clout.

A princess, I said, what's that?

Wears a crown. Kisses the frog.

I know *that.* But—

She's a part of the court, Promise said. Think maid of honor. Think second best with high hopes. A princess is smart or popular but not beautiful like the queen. Weren't you in high school?

I can't see you as a princess, I said. At some private school in Manhattan?

Public school, she said, and this was in Connecticut. Anyway, I was a more-than-willing participant. I was usually the instigator. All I needed was a couch at some boy's house, the parents upstairs watching television or diddling on the computer, and everything could get kissy in a hurry. It seems a little stupid now. My oral phase.

— —

Jeffrey Dahmer? My god, Bob, have I eaten you? Have I sexually assaulted you?

That's not the point, he said. You've taken some private fantasy and enacted it. Healthy people, if I can call them that, don't enact their little fantasies. Their fantasies stay fantasies.

You?

Me? Me *what*?

Do you have fantasies?

Of course I do, Bob said. But I don't—

What kind of fantasies?

The same ones you have.

I doubt that, Bob.

Acting on them is another matter entirely, he said. It means you've forgotten the difference between fantasy and real life. This is real life, Evan. My name's Bob Partnow. I have a job I need to get back to. My authors are wondering where the hell I am. I've been sitting in a cage for nine days. And you're Evan Ulmer, and you have the key. I mean, who are we kidding here? You thought this would be an interesting little experiment? Let's be honest, Evan.

I took a deep breath and felt the kind of disappointment only an abductor can feel in the face of his unhappy captive. Hadn't there been any good times? Hadn't Bob gotten anything out of the experience? If nothing else, hadn't he lost a few pounds, gotten some rest, seen himself become a minor celebrity in the popular press? I could've gone down that road—pointing out the advantages, putting the best face on things—but what was the use? Obviously Bob wasn't in the mood for silver linings. Already he'd pegged me for a Jeffrey Dahmer.

You cheat on your wife and you're worried about *my* fantasies?

I don't cheat on my wife, Bob said.

What, Claudia knows and doesn't care?

More or less, Bob said—shrugging, and surprising me.

What happens in the fantasies?

What fantasies?

You said you had fantasies, I said.

What happens? Bob said. I'll tell you. I get out of this cage and maybe I drag your ass in here and—

And what? I said. Do you sodomize me? Jesus, Bob, is that what this is all about?

— ▬

I never intended to be the captor I'd become—less cockeyed master than honorable servant. I mean, wasn't it reasonable to assume that abducting a person and then caging him would turn you into an animal yourself—losing your mind, going over the edge?

That wasn't how it was happening. Sometimes, especially on those days when I never set foot in the library or got around to writing in my notebooks, Bob and his situation reminded me of the plight of some fictional character I'd created. I had to worry over him and prompt him, like any other reluctant pawn of narrative.

Maybe I was naïve, but it did surprise me—the sheer responsibility involved in keeping someone holed up.

— ▬

After giving *Dateline* five minutes of our attention, Bob and I watched a segment on CNN dealing with what the thin-lipped, button-nosed blonde commentator called "the ongoing saga of Robert Partnow's disappearance."

Saga? That struck me as a bit sensational. The local news had already spoken of the disappearance in equally dramatic terms, with breathy mentions of sexual scandal and the homosexual underworld, but that was all you expected, even secretly wanted, from local news.

Bob watched silently as the blonde spoke of a Princeton education and a "methodical rise to the upper echelons of trade publishing"; and then we were offered still pictures of the editor's wife and two daughters. (The latter were news to me, though I confess I hadn't thought of asking.) And then we watched filmed footage of "a florist purported to be having an affair with Mr. Partnow at the time of the abduction." Lloyd looked a little too upbeat for the segment—striding across a street, dodging a taxi, popping open an umbrella with a flourish of his left hand. I recognized the corner as one I sometimes passed in Little Italy. Fleeing the camera's attention, his movements fluid, Lloyd was oddly photogenic. It almost seemed set up, this shot—like footage from a mock documentary.

That's not true, Bob said—staring at the screen as the image of Lloyd gave way to a photograph of Claudia, her long red hair pulled back into a ponytail. Compensating for the lesser medium, the camera swooped in on the photographed face to reveal a cover of freckles.

What's not true?

I wasn't having an affair with Lloyd at the time.

I thought—

I'd been having an affair with Lloyd, if that's what you want to call it, for two years. That's hardly *at the time.*

I looked at Bob, but his eyes were glued to the television screen as the segment was winding down with a final image of Bob shrinking to a rectangle in the corner of the screen behind Kyra Phillips, our anchor.

Is it nice seeing Lloyd?

It's strange, Bob said—softly now, almost absentmindedly, looking in my direction; he wasn't so much staring at me as through me. He doesn't look like Lloyd, he said. I mean, I've never seen Lloyd on television. He looks—

He looks—

He looks almost angelic, Bob said. A little fatuous, too.

Better that than fat, I said—a comment that made Bob's eyes suddenly focus on mine.

By the time we returned our gaze to the television, the news had moved on—the screen jumping with images of people shooting guns at other people in a third-world urban setting. A male voice now spoke gravely of "the international community" and "the inevitable repercussions."

—‑—

Maybe I was naïve, but it did surprise me—the sheer responsibility involved in keeping someone holed up. Not only did I have to prepare food and provide clothes and wash linens and supply toilet paper and Q-tips and dark blue bottles of Milk of Magnesia, but I also had to weather my abductee's moods and shield my eyes during the sponge baths. Sometimes it felt like having a dog or a cat—my only previous experiment in selflessness. (I'm not counting my last days with my mother, since selflessness wasn't really involved there.) Or, because I also had to put up with complaints and gauge their relative merits, it often felt like being a parent. And I did experience that strange seesaw I'd heard about—daily drudgery edging up to moments of subtle drama and humor. (Witness my exuberance whenever I saw Bob getting on the treadmill without even a nudge.)

A good plan, I told myself—mimicking the voice of my father—is one that adapts. Success in this scheme, like any other, was a matter of walking the tightrope between a plan going astray and a plan too rigid to accommodate the unforeseeable. Was I following in *his* footsteps? My father was drawn to plans that assumed a responsibility toward the future. He also tended to worry about others, to show sympathy, only after having taken steps that were *detrimental to the well-being of another person* (as Bob put it one day, officiously, in describing my injurious actions).

I did worry. Everything now was troubling me—Bob's stomach problems, his migraines, the melancholy effect of reading and rereading his little stack of news stories about himself. (Should I have taken those away from him—as a parent of a small child might a sharp object?) I worried about his loneliness, about the trauma of his parents' divorce when he was twelve, about the strain of his double life with his wife and Lloyd. What must that have been like? And did Bob stay with his wife out of love, out of misplaced loyalty, out of a desire not to inflict on his daughters the same trauma once inflicted on him? How easy could it be, after all, to be Robert Partnow at this moment—anticipating a dramatic return to his messy world?

4

Love is one thing. But drama, that slithery seductress in my head—she's always told a different story. Not the drama of what you'll find in today's mail, or whether the dog pissed on the rug again. Not the events of a Monday or a Wednesday, but the whole hullabaloo of drama—big drama—unfurling. For that kind of drama, you have to turn on the television or flip the pages of a magazine to find a celebrity or a politician (or a writer?) who has a private life that's public.

What's Julia Roberts doing right now, at this very moment? Chatting with husband Danny? Clipping her toenails? Interviewing nannies? Thinking back on Kiefer, Lyle, Liam, Benjamin? Reading, lounging poolside, allowing herself to be courted by the latest script? Where is Julia? What is she thinking, what's bugging her today?

I've never been able to shake the desire to serve as source of public wonder, to be loved by thousands if not millions, to have others weakened by their curiosity. What's the thing with Evan Ulmer? What's he up to? *Someone wants to know, someone other than your relatives and meager coterie of friends who have nothing better to sit around and wonder about.*

It sometimes boggles the mind—OK, my *mind—to think that there's only one. One Julia Roberts. A single god at a distance, a voice in the wilderness that beckons you toward a charmed life that will never be yours. How can there be only one when she seems to be everywhere at once—in magazines, on television, in the movies, in the dreams of one hundred and twenty-three Americans each night, on average? Somehow, one doesn't seem the proper number. One is some loser—lonely in his lonely world, with another loser who loves him only because life has dealt her the same lousy hand.*

There is only one Evan Ulmer, for example. Is there supposed to be consolation in that?

ALMOST TWO WEEKS into the abduction scenario, Bob and I had pretty much fallen into the habit of watching television every evening. Partly to keep tabs on the story (*our* story, as I thought of it), but mostly just for the fun of it. (So much for books, literature, the whole *raison d'être* of publishing.) Sometimes Bob watched television while he worked out on the treadmill; but often he just sat in his chair, on his side of the fence, while I sat in mine, on mine. We were like a family in that way—comforted by the warmth of the television's special glow, the sameness of the flickering images. And when I thought about it—usually during commercial breaks, while staring absently at the so-called library I'd constructed for Bob—the act of reading did seem awfully solipsistic.

It was always a news show of one kind or another—straight news, weekly news magazines, commentary on the news. Occasionally, on slow evenings, we turned to *Court TV* or the melodrama of *Cops* or reruns of *Oprah* or the latest, tired examples of reality TV. Once or twice we watched the newest incarnation of *Divorce Court,* which prompted Bob's confession of his parents' split and its emotional impact. (When he asked me about my parents, I spoke of divorce as a wish that had never materialized.) We very rarely watched a sitcom or a dramatic series.

We had different philosophies of channel selection. I liked to switch channels often, on the theory that something good was always just around the corner. Bob's faith worked differently—he preferred to give things a chance, wade through commercials, and simply wait. When I bought a second remote control, it became possible for either of us to trump the other's choice by hitting the UP or DOWN button. There were incidents where the channel would go up a step, then down a step, then up a step, and so on— engaged in a war of remotes, our respective eyes resolutely fixed on the screen. But eventually, we settled on a more humane system. I took pleasure in these acts of coordination; and I think Bob did, too—though I never asked.

Once, more as an experiment than a provocation, I placed the edge of a wrench on my remote control and sent the television on a steady wild goose chase through the cable channels. With each channel displaying itself for a single second before giving way to the next, the parade of programs held no hidden narrative that either of us could fathom. Nonetheless I loved it, this scramble of images. Indulging me, Bob commented on the huge percentage of television shows that involved someone looking directly at you—talking, imploring, explaining. And he was right. In another world, it might've passed for eye contact.

— —

Where do you get your ideas? I asked Promise, looking down and zipping up my jacket. We were sitting on a green bench in the park in downtown Sandhurst. Two weeks into May, it was uncommonly chilly.

For fiction? she said. I wish I knew. They come in bunches, or they don't come at all. Right now I'm in a dead period.

Do you ever take things from real life?

What do you mean, *real life*?

— —

It took me awhile to figure it out, to bite at the bait—but Bob had gotten into the practice of tracking the days, slipping the exact number into our conversations as though to remind me of my deepening criminality. Knowing about my past religiosity, he was probably guessing I was the kind of ex-believer who made distinctions based on a sin's longevity. Obviously he wasn't familiar with my Presbyterian upbringing—the latitude of predestination, the guise of faith, and other quagmires of dogma.

In any case, I did appreciate Bob's keeping count. I'd never been

good at math. I'd never got around to hanging calendars on the wall
or attaching them to the refrigerator door—or whatever it is that
most people do to take notice of the passing days.

—　—

What do you mean, *real life?*

This, for example, I said—releasing my eyes from Promise's,
motioning with my hand and looking around the park. On the
other side of the walkway, children played in the sandbox while
mothers and nannies watched and gossiped. One child, a girl wearing a heavy yellow slicker, was trying in vain to dig a hole with a pink
plastic shovel. Repeatedly the shovel fell from her hand, and each
time, before picking it up, she stared down at it—surprised by its
sudden appearance at her feet.

I'm bad at description, Promise said. I once tried to describe my
dog, just as an exercise—

You have a dog?

Hans, yes. And it was hopeless. I'm bad, bad, bad at description.
And you'd think I might be good. I do believe in writing about
things right in front of me, using them as inspiration. Did I ever tell
you I once painted?

No.

Mostly still lifes, she said—making a motion in the air with
an imaginary brush. Maybe I'll do some more when I get back to
New York. Anyway, I still work that way at writing sometimes. I
put something in front of me, something real, an odd brooch or a
picture of my mother, and I write about it. I *use* it, but I never really
write to describe it. I'm bad at description.

What are you good at?

She smiled at me, her lips curling. There was something strange
about her smile, though I couldn't quite put my finger on it. I'd
meant the question seriously, but I found myself looking at her—at
her smile, at her mouth, since that's where her smile *was*, where it
resided; and my focus got lost, momentarily, and my head began to

spin just a little; and I can't say I moved my mouth any closer to her mouth, but neither can I say I wasn't the one who initiated the kiss. It *was* my doing.

At first the kiss itself got a little lost. Once our lips touched, and our tongues found each other—like lovers' hands in a dark cave—my mind returned to its doubting ways and I wondered, right then and there, whether I was like all the others who'd already been there. (Was she still in her oral phase, gunning for another boy?) Then again, it really didn't matter where her consent came from. And once my mind relaxed, I was able to feel the kiss—now in the middle of achieving a long, extended life of its own. Most of all it felt warm, even hot, perhaps because of the cold weather. And yes, she *was* good at it. (*Practice makes perfect,* my father used to say, proudly, as though he'd yet again happened upon the phrase himself.) Any kiss is a mutual rehearsal, but here, more so than usual, she was feeding me the lines; and, following her cues, I was improvising as best I could.

Finally, we pulled apart.

Hello, she said—as if we'd just then been introduced by a mutual friend.

Hi.

And we smiled at each other until we looked toward the sandbox again.

— —

So you've had agents.

Two, I said.

Well, that's good news right there, Bob said—pushing the button on the treadmill and beginning to walk.

Two is better than one?

No, but—

You thought I was a total loser, I said—and for a moment, leaning into the chain-link fence, I considered what it would be like to be *less* successful.

What I meant—

No, Bob, I'm the guy who gets the agent and then the agent tries to sell the book and it doesn't sell and so then the agent says good-bye, good luck, it's been sweet knowing you.

You haven't found the right agent, he said—in the strange, elevated tone of a sanguine broadcaster. Or maybe the book hasn't gotten itself in the hands of a good line editor. It's sort of a catch-22 that way. These things don't happen automatically. It's never easy.

Monica Sanchez, I said—popping the name, and watching carefully for Bob's reaction.

She's a very good agent. I know her.

Yes, and she knows you. She's the one who got my book to you.

Monica, he said—a bewildered look on his face as he stared straight ahead, working his thin calves, his ballooning thighs. She's your agent?

Was. Keep your tenses straight.

And I read your book? A little out of breath, he asked the question in an almost imploring voice—soft and tentative and spoken as though to a child. *And do you like your new teddy bear?* I could barely hear him over the steady thrum of the treadmill.

Did you think—

You waited this long to tell me?

You thought I just pulled your name out of a hat?

What did I say about it? Bob said. About your manuscript. In my—

In your gracious letter of rejection? You know, compliments on the writing, on the interior world of the protagonist. Then you complained about the insularity of the viewpoint and how, in a formal sense, the novel suffered from the agoraphobic flavor of its topic. Thank you so much for showing us your work. Sincerely, Mr. Robert Partnow. Monica waited a good three weeks and told me it was time for me to seek other representation.

I'm sorry, Bob said.

After clearing my throat, I looked off toward the refrigerator in the corner—exactly half the capacity of the normal size but twice as efficient, or so said the guy at Appliance City. Bob's black leather satchel was still sitting on top.

To be honest, Evan, I don't remember the book. Tell me what it's about.

A woman suffers from agoraphobia. She lives in Milwaukee. She owns a monkey.

Yes, Bob said—nodding his head as he continued his stride, going nowhere on the treadmill. I remember Milwaukee, the monkey.

The monkey's name was Cecil.

I didn't read it. Melanie, one of my assistants, read it. And we talked about it.

Bob increased the speed of the treadmill—remembering my manuscript seemed to put him on edge. Did he want to get away from me? It was still a paltry pace, even a minute or two into his routine, and it struck me that Bob hadn't gotten used to pain, probably never would. Maybe he was exercising a little more, but was he feeling the sting? Did he have any sense of how many pounds he had to go?

How long did you talk about it? This Melanie and you.

Well, probably—

Be honest, I said.

OK, I'll *be* honest. A couple of minutes. Five minutes maybe.

What was the point of talking about it?

It's our procedure. I hear her report. Melanie's report, in this case. I have a written copy, of course, but—

How long was the report?

It's usually no longer than half a page, he said—sounding winded now. Unless we're very interested. Unless our decision is unusually difficult.

So she wrote the report and—

She presented it to me. Orally.

The letter? I asked.

She probably wrote the letter. I signed it.

Did you read the letter?

Of course I read the letter, Bob said—reaching for a hand towel to blot his forehead.

You're lying, I said.

I'm *not,* he said—looking over at me. I never sign a letter I haven't read.

The manuscript, Bob. You never read it. Melanie never read it.

She may've skimmed over a few—

I never sent you the manuscript, I said—waving my arms in front of him, as though trying to get a car to slow down on a lonely road.

You just told me—

I know what I told you. I made it up.

So then *you're* lying.

Yes, Bob, in a sense that's true.

Did you even write a novel?

Set in Milwaukee, with a monkey named Cecil? What do you think?

— —

And we smiled at each other until we looked toward the sand-box again. I couldn't help wondering, as is my way, whether the children—or, more to the point, their keepers—had seen our kiss.

If you're not good at description, I asked—returning to our original topic—what *are* you good at?

As a writer? Promise said. Dialogue, mostly. Sometimes interior thought. Maybe I should move to Amherst and become a spinster poet. What are you good at?

Apparently not enough, I said—hesitating for a moment, teetering on the edge of disclosure. I find it difficult just doing the work.

Day to day, you mean.

Yes, I said. I've had a mild case of writing block for a long, long time. Until just recently, in fact. Sometimes not so mild.

And what are you writing now? Promise asked—and quickly she

moved toward me, across the slight distance between us on the park bench, to kiss me on the cheek. She did it quickly, almost furtively, as though she were getting away with something. It made me think of the shoplifting.

I've just started something, I said—smiling at her. A story. Maybe a novel.

What's it about? she asked—then laughed and shook her head. That's a stupid question, I know. Sorry. My mother and her friends ask me that question and I never know what to say.

I'm writing about a man who abducts another man, I said—realizing, as I said it, that it sounded almost generic; not exactly the oldest story ever told, but close. *Loser abducts winner and tries to steal the magic.* The epiphany? *There is no magic, only perseverance.* He keeps him in his basement, I said. In a cage.

Like an animal, she said—nodding her head.

It's a big cage. More like a jail, a prison. With a treadmill for exercise, and one of those bathrooms. The plastic thing.

A Porta-Potty?

Yes, that's it, I said—and this, her quirky knowledge, meant as much as her furtive kiss a half-minute earlier.

Why?

— —

So what's it like?

Why do you ask? Bob said. Are you interested?

Are you interested in me being interested?

Bob shook his head, rolled his eyes, lowered the opened *Newsweek* to his lap. Upside down, its cover showed a woman in a white lab coat, wearing protective goggles, holding up an everyday kitchen sponge with a pair of tongs. "Silent Killers," the cover announced—I could see it, twisting my head.

Sex with a man instead of a woman, Bob said. That's what it's like. There's nothing particularly earth-shattering about the difference. At least for me. In fact, I wish I could say there was more of a difference.

But then you're bisexual, I said.

I guess so.

You guess so?

Mostly it doesn't feel that way, Bob said. It feels more like being homosexual *and* heterosexual, both of them separately. Not both at the same time. It's hard to explain. I'm a divided man.

Join the club, I said—thinking of mental division and my own three hundred and seventeen contradictions, including my capacity to converse enjoyably and intimately with a detainee in a cage of chain-link fence sunk in concrete. I wasn't above appreciating the strangeness of the situation.

What about you? Bob said. Where's your sexuality aimed?

This was, I thought, an odd way of putting it. Does one aim one's sexuality? Bob's question made me think more of weapons than women. And first it brought to mind an image of a gun held to my own head; and then the image morphed, a finger replacing the gun—an everyday gesture directed at you to remind you to think before acting. *Don't be dumb now.* I recognized it as my father's favorite form of censure. Pushed to the brink of exasperation by his teenage son, he'd had this habit—angrily pointing a finger to his own head, trying to conjure in me the power of common sense. *Think.*

These days it's aimed mostly at myself, I finally said.

Bob nodded, and I took this as acknowledgment of the wisdom of being self-reliant when up against a wall—professionally or romantically. It wasn't quite true, of course—or not completely; but I relied, in making my statement, on the long days, the many years, when no one else was aiming anything at me, unless you counted stares of indifference.

— —

Why?

Why what?

Why does the man kidnap the other man?

He doesn't really kidnap him, I said. It's more an abduction. Didn't you ever want to abduct somebody?

I don't think so, Promise said—her dark hair pendulous as she turned to look at the sandbox, at the girl with the loose hand and pink shovel. I used to think a lot about kidnapping when I was a kid, but it was always the other way around. I must've read something in the newspaper. Some weird guy abducts me and won't let me go, and I get older and older. My mother eventually gives up and turns my room into the pretentious study she's always wanted. And then finally I get away.

How?

I don't remember. I act charming, forgive him. Fool him into trusting me or something. Then stick a knife in his fucking eye.

I imagined the pain—an eyeball, severed almost completely by a kitchen knife. Cradled in the cup of my hand, hanging by a gelatinous thread. Which would be worse, the pain or the idea of being betrayed by Promise?

Did you read in the paper—

Would it be so bad to be abducted? I asked. As an adult, I mean. And if the guy wasn't some weirdo and you were allowed to read a lot of books and get writing done and watch television and whatnot.

Is that what happens in your novel?

It's more a novella.

Sounds like that movie, she said. Sounds like *The King of Comedy*. My parents' all-time favorite movie. Jerry Lewis.

Yes, right, and Robert De Niro, I said—smiling for no reason, trying to *not* feel insulted. She might as well have said, *I once had a boyfriend who looked just like you.*

Maybe you should abduct me, Promise said. You know, to get a sense of what it would be like.

Is that an invitation?

Just a thought, she said. I'm a big believer in experience.

Writing what you know, I said—enunciating the words but mostly watching Promise, waiting for her to respond.

What are you looking at? she asked—frowning, looking down, forcing her eyes to cross.

Your mouth. I was just watching your mouth form the words.
Your tongue, really.

Naughty boy.

The words came out quickly, and so at first I thought she'd said
not a boy. Maybe it was that Promise didn't strike me as the kind of
girl who would use the word *naughty*.

Can I ask you a question? she said. Yes, OK, I know, now I've
already asked you a question.

Ask away.

Actually I have *two* questions. Can I ask two?

As though to coax me into agreeing, Promise smiled. And I
realized then what it was about her smile—it was mostly her eyes
that did the smiling; the edges of her mouth moved upward, and
her ample lips poked out, but it was her eyes that underwent the
real transformation. She squeezed the outside corners, almost in a
parody of pain.

First question demands a quick response, she said. Did you kiss
me for a reason?

A reason? I said—buying a little time. Yes, I did. Because I
wanted to. Because I *have* wanted to. And I was tired of worrying
about whether you wanted to. Too.

The fatigue of it, she said—nodding, then smiling again. And so
what's the kidnapper's motivation?

Is that your second question?

Yes. In your novel, I mean.

That's the part I can't figure out, I said. And it's sort of driving
me crazy.

— ◆ —

You know, I once had my own aspirations, Bob said.

I've never thought of you as being a man *without* aspirations,
I said.

I'm talking about writing.

Writing?

Being a writer, he said—pointing at me. Like you.

You wrote?

I tried, he said. That was the original plan, straight out of college. I was editor of a small literary magazine at Princeton. At the time I had ambitions of becoming a novelist.

What happened?

I moved to New York City and sat in an apartment and stared at a blank piece of paper for weeks. And then, predictably, I moved into the world of publishing. *Fell* into it. You know—

The accidental profession.

Right. Yes. It's not a very original story.

I thought of that, I said, once or twice. Becoming an editorial assistant. Getting a foot in the door.

You see, Bob said. We have something in common.

Believe it or not, legal proofreading paid better.

I believe it.

— —

In Dr. Mendelssohn's office on Twelfth Street below Chelsea, I spoke of headaches and a drug I'd heard about and my sister and how the drug had worked remarkably well on *her* migraines. I was hoping I'd never mentioned siblings before, or the lack thereof. The doctor nodded, closing his eyes momentarily. Out of annoyance? No, I immediately saw—it was empathy. He had tufts of white hair growing off the top ridges of both ears. Was this new, or had I just never noticed it before?

How are you otherwise? Dr. Mendelssohn asked.

Good.

The depression—

Gone, I said—trying not to sound triumphant. Triumphantly overcoming depression was, I worried, a sign of relapse. I was thinking on my feet, trying to hold it together, performing in my own private movie.

That's good, he said. Nothing wrong with that. And how's Sandhurst?

Slow. Beautiful.

I keep thinking about buying there. My wife prefers the Hamptons. The kids prefer the Hamptons.

There's the beach, I said—shrugging.

So, just as soon as you see the flicker, he said—returning to his professional role, jiggling his fountain pen in front of my eyes—be sure to take the Imitrex. That should do the trick.

Thanks.

These are entirely new? The migraines?

When I was a kid I had them, and then they went away, I said—trying to remember. Hadn't this been what Bob had said? His early years as an editor, the terrible eyestrain from too much reading, the paradox of it never causing him headaches. Then, out of nowhere, they'd returned.

Childhood has a way of doing that, sneaking up on you, Dr. Mendelssohn said—keeping his eyes on me as he reached, like clockwork, and slipped the pen into the pocket of his smock.

Once outside, crossing Fourteenth and walking north into Chelsea, I couldn't help but imagine I was Robert Partnow. It was like coming out of a movie, facing the glare of daylight, and envisioning yourself as the larger-than-life protagonist. I put the best spin on things; I monkeyed a little with the truth. A new prescription for a migraine medication in my pocket, a successful career in tow, famous authors on speed dial, not to mention a wife and someone named Lloyd who broke the boredom, I walked and crossed streets purposefully. Yes, life was messy, but it had its upside, and redemption—a staple of *successful storytelling,* Bob had said—was never far away. Having watched him on the treadmill, I knew that he had a little jig in his step—his heel rose an inch or two at the last possible moment, just when you thought it had reached its crest—and I tried to emulate it. I tried to locate the jig's source.

On the train back to Sandhurst, I was again more or less my-self. (Usually a sign of mental health—just not in my case.) And I couldn't keep myself from thinking about Promise—her tongue, her mouth, and the rest of her body stretching out in my mind like an unwieldy map of desire. I was, I realized, intimidated. Scared.

— —

You're everywhere, I said.

I slipped the rolled-up magazine through a square of the chain-link fence. Once, way back when, I'd considered shielding Bob from outside news of his situation. But for what purpose? If nothing else, we shared a lust for news, a faith in the possibility that today would be nothing like yesterday. There was always the thrill of *developments*. Reading about himself, following his own story, must've doubled or tripled the thrill. How was I to compete with a fictional account of an abduction, especially given Bob's criteria of salable storytelling? Didn't reality have a way of making fiction seem like an act of des-peration—like french kissing your mother on a lonely night?

Everywhere? Bob said. No, I'm right here. In this musty dun-geon. Have been for sixteen days.

I bristled a little at Bob's characterization. A dungeon, perhaps. It was the reference to *musty* that bothered me, especially after I'd gone to the trouble of buying and burning four aromatic candles and setting a couple of dehumidifiers on high to deal with a smell that my own nose couldn't sense. What else could I do?

What is it? Bob asked—reaching for the magazine.

People. There's a little story on Lloyd. A picture of him in a bright red sweater, sitting in his living room with a rodent of a dog and enough flowers in garish vases to make just about anyone cringe.

Evan, remember, Bob said—stopping first to peruse the cover, which announced another Hollywood breakup—real men don't cringe. Her name's Bixie and she's a pug. You have a problem with red sweaters?

He looks like every wife's nightmare, I said.

5

*And so, yes, the burden of my father's dismissive attitude toward
my career was gone; but very soon I felt even more pressure. No
longer employed, I had ample time to write—for the first time
since graduate school. But was I? Was I writing? During those
last days in New York, and now in Sandhurst, did I ever write
more than a dribble?*

*After my parents died, my own timidity became unavoid-
able—it was jammed right under my nose. And it was depressing. (My timidity, not my parents' deaths.) I couldn't help
feeling downcast, on the brink of disappearing or at least trudging around the rest of my life with severely weighted shoulders.
And it made me long for escape. I had this sense of being on one
of those wobbly, wooden bridges—like in a Tarzan movie, or
in some nightmarish jungle—and it was coming apart right
under my feet, and I had to hurry to make it to the other side. It
made me want to run somewhere, anywhere.*

*As it turned out, I made my way across the George Washing-
ton Bridge. The day I rented the car and went across that bridge,
north of the city, I'd never even heard of Sandhurst. I'm taking
two days off—a trip to the country, I told myself. But in the
back rooms of my mind, where most everything gets adjudicated,
I must've had fantasies of getting away on a more permanent
basis. It was time to do something new—something drastic, even.*

*Sandhurst wasn't perfect, but its stillness reminded me a
little of my boyhood. OK, it wasn't Appleton, Wisconsin, but
it wasn't New York City either. And so I stayed a week at the
Sandhurst Inn, reading books in my room and venturing out
on hilly walks for which I had no shoes. On the second day, I
went into a dinky real-estate office, met an agent. She had a
slight limp from a recent automobile accident, and so I insisted
on doing the driving. We took her Dodge Durango and looked
at ten or so houses before I found one that I could afford. I acted
quickly, paying with the money my mother had left me.*

Bob could be moody. I was finding this out. And whether I'd prompted Bob's moodiness or merely come to recognize it, the abduction scenario began to slip in my mind as a means of self-aggrandizement. I was becoming too sensitive to Bob's opinion of me—or at least inept at hiding my thoughts. I felt pressured, for instance, into showing him more of my writing, if only because he kept asking. And it pained me to know that what he thought of me couldn't be separated from our relationship as abductee and abductor. It seemed a shame, but there it was—a relationship defined in the most narrow of terms.

Bob would've probably scoffed at this, but I did want to help him. Maybe at the time, on that fateful April day in Manhattan, I hadn't really thought of it that way. But very quickly I realized that I not only expected Bob to savor this respite, this breather from the onslaught of mediocre manuscripts and pushy authors; I also wanted him to be happy—and this, obviously, before I even knew what a challenge this would be.

In an effort to inspire him, I once mentioned to Bob the possibility of writing a memoir—*Heady Days of an Abductee,* a working title. It might be good for him to revisit old aspirations, give prose another try in a slightly different genre. After all, as Bob knew better than I did, the memoir craze was now an industry in itself. But Bob resisted the idea, saying he was now and forever an editor, not a writer—and, by the way, when exactly was I was going to let him go? As though writers were the only ones held captive by ambition.

— —

And how's that little guy in the basement? Promise asked at the end of a long phone conversation. We'd been talking, more or less abstractly, about the beginnings and endings of stories and novels, and how middles were too often middling.

He's fine, I said. He's a little tired of sitting around in the basement.

In his cage. No, no, it's really a jail, right?

A cage, a jail. One or the other.

Does he have a name?

Not yet, I said.

What about the other guy?

I'm calling him K. Just for the time being.

Franz might not approve, Promise said—clucking her tongue. Franz was more than a little proprietary, you know. Especially with his fiancées. Paranoid, too. So he's not out yet?

Out?

Of the basement.

No, he's still there. Stuck in a plot going nowhere, I think. I mean, what's the point? Why was he abducted in the first place?

Motivation, she said. Don't you just hate it?

— —

Bob sat motionless in the straight-backed chair, a few inches from the television. *He makes people laugh for a living, but for his whole life David Spade has felt the dark pull of depression. In an exclusive interview, David tells Diane Sawyer how he wrestled with depression and at last overcame it.*

OK, here, listen, he suddenly said—lowering the volume. Let's start over. You think you should be published, right?

From my side of the fence I blew out a sigh and then shrugged. We'd already been down this road, endlessly reciting the lines from some bad Hollywood script about artistic disappointment.

I mean, as much as the next guy, he said.

You know what I think.

Then I cleared my throat and looked away from Bob—toward the screen and its images of Diane Sawyer looking earnest in a studio setting. And for a long moment we sat silent. I didn't really want to have another conversation about me. Instead I looked at the television, its shifting images; and I was thinking about how the problem with life was that you couldn't turn it off. Only the outward voice. That annoying rabble of mine, the wag of my own tongue—that could be cut off, but how exactly would that help? The most biting comments, the ones I made about myself, never so much as roused my tongue.

I may not be a genius, I said, but I deserve a place at the table. That's all.

Yes, right, Bob said. And that's called ambition. You can't get anywhere without it. But do you have any idea how many writers in America, let alone the whole world, think they deserve a place at that table? Do you know how many manuscripts come into my office, just *my* office, in a single day?

Thousands.

I know all about struggling writers, Bob said—suddenly standing up, giving his back a stretch. I was once one myself.

Oh please, that's not fair, I said—annoyed at this pretense at empathy. You weren't a writer. You were—

That's not my point, Evan. My point is that I'm in a position to know. Especially in my younger days, I dealt with these people all the time. And you know how many bust their asses and never get anywhere? Have you thought about that? I mean, you can't think you're a special case.

A one-of-a-kind failure? I said. No, there's no such thing. Failure is a thousand times more likely than success. What *is* failure?

You're asking me? Bob said.

Failure is the strongest creature in the jungle, I said—a little too loudly, already ashamed of the analogy. Failure's the almighty cockroach of life. It's inevitable, I know that. And do I deserve failure? Am I untalented? Am I a loser whose only claim to fame is the persistence of my stupidity? Was it worse than stupid to abduct you, Robert Partnow, and follow in the footsteps of other slacker sociopaths? I ask myself those questions. How often? All the time.

My words had come out in a rush, and immediately I regretted their fervor. I looked at Bob, directly through the fence, and he was looking back at me with raised eyebrows. I was beginning to tell him too much. Bad enough to have these thoughts myself without parading them in front of a captive audience. Wasn't it best to shift topics, move our conversation toward the psychology of the abductee?

Bob, do you realize what you've never asked me? I don't think there's been even once—

Asked you what?

To let you go. *Please stop the car, let me out!*

I was driving.

Exactly my point, Bob. Whether you know it or not, you made it very easy for someone like me, a mere amateur. And all along, you've never really demanded your release. Isn't that weird?

What are you talking about?

Not really, I said. You did once touch on the idea that—

Oh, *that's* why I'm still here, Bob said—frowning, throwing his arms up, rocking back on his heels, and doing an imitation of sudden insight.

I'm not suggesting you don't *want* to go.

Should I put my request in writing? he said. Would that help? Would that—

No need to get angry, Bob. I was just asking. You know, whether you thought it was weird.

— —

I don't know, I said—over the phone. My mind's not coming up with anyone.

Just someone you could never kiss, Promise said. You can have me, right, but what about—

What about Nicole Kidman? Will she work?

You like her?

Shouldn't I?

I'm just asking, she said. OK, so you go down to Food Town and suddenly there's Nicole, coming down your aisle. And she's reaching for some salad dressing, Thousand Island, and then accidentally drops the bottle, and it spills all over your shoes. And so she apologizes and she wipes your shoes with a handkerchief that she pulls out of her purse. And then she offers to have coffee with you, and you end up going to Java Junction. And you talk. And she says she'd like to see you again.

This wouldn't be happening, I said.

But it *is,* Promise said. It *is* happening to you, and that's the point. And now she wants to see you again.

See me again? See me again *how*?

Just what it sounds like, Evan. It's gotten a little romantic, at least in Nicole's mind. She wants to see you again, even though—

Even though I'm with you.

Exactly, she said. And so now what do you do?

— —

Lloyd?

No, Bob said. Claudia.

And why?

Have you ever been married?

No, I said—wondering whether Bob meant the question seriously.

She's a stabilizing force, he said. She keeps me alive.

Are you afraid of dying?

I'm not particularly afraid of you, if that's what you mean. Which might be foolish of me. I mean, who am I kidding? Maybe you've brainwashed me, Evan.

No, I said—thinking how nice it would be to cleanse my own brain, like taking a hose to a dog come home from a wild, muddy escapade.

Who knows what you might do, he said. But I don't worry that you're going to take my life.

I threw the gun away.

Well, OK. I mean, maybe you did and maybe you didn't.

I did, I said. Have you seen the gun recently?

I only saw it once, Bob said. I haven't seen it since. But then it's not like I've been given the run of the house.

— —

Every few days there was another news story about Bob's disappearance. These stories made no mention of me. With each article, there was a picture of Bob—often the same one I'd cut out of *Publishers Weekly*. Or sometimes, if the rag was published in color, the picture made Robert Partnow look like a dashing, rosy-cheeked figure; you could imagine his wife loving him, as she claimed, no less for having discovered his homosexual exploits. Once or twice I'd spied a small smile on Bob's face as he scrutinized this very same picture.

The frequency of the articles seemed to increase. It was easy to imagine reporters making phone calls, running down leads, fitting facts together or working bravely in their absence. Under these circumstances gossip was, of course, inevitable. The *New York Observer,* never quiet for long, had written in detail about the reactions of editors at rival houses (with less-impressive lists of authors). A few of Bob's colleagues claimed off the record to have seen problems coming, at least in regard to Lloyd and Claudia and what the headline called SEPARATE WORLDS COLLIDING. *Time* had a small article that, playing off of a longer list of recent scandals in the world of publishing, spun the idea that literary professionalism had lost some of its sheen. An article in *Newsweek* took a step back and worked the media-coverage angle, drawing the dramatic arch—how Bob had been initially maligned by the assumption that his closeted homosexuality might've had something to do with the kidnapping.

I wasn't above noticing that I'd become even more invisible as a result of Robert Partnow's rise to prominence; I was absent from the compelling story of his plight and those who loved him, missed him, and prayed for his return. It was one of those little paradoxes of anonymous criminality. And increasingly, it seemed, Bob was becoming an object of sympathy. Even the police, now keen on the intricacies of the publishing industry, seemed certain that the abduction was likely an expression of authorial anger.

But whose anger, and how much of an author was he?

— —

Have you been writing much, Evan?

I was standing on the other side of the fence, pleased again that Bob had gotten on the treadmill.

Writing? I said—looking over toward the television screen, which was oddly blank for once. Wow, that comes out of the blue. Why are you asking?

Just curious, Bob said—reaching out and upping the speed of the treadmill.

Not lately.

It was at moments like these that I felt almost dizzy, excited and scared and very much beyond the project of lying. But Bob said nothing and continued his morning jog. Had he guessed? Or was he as gullible as I wanted him to be? Or maybe what I really wanted was for him *not* to be gullible. What if he saw through me, understood me, what if his watchful eye made it impossible for me to keep any secrets?

I was feeling closer to Bob, and he was starting to get under my skin in ways I couldn't explain to myself. For one thing, I was beginning to ask myself a lot of questions. Was that a good sign? A bad sign?

— —

Maybe we should go to the park, I said—from my side of the library table.

With my voice an unsteady whisper, I felt like the timid soul who *always* waits for the green light before crossing the street.

Evan, Promise said—my name suddenly a plea.

Even if it was raining sheets, I did think a walk might be fun. It would allow us to get away from the library, from the gaze of the librarian, from the scent of books and blamelessness. But Promise was intent on returning to the scene of our original meeting—*the stacks*. I had a little trouble with that term, the way she kept using it, because it didn't really apply to a library of this size. Maybe at Yale there were stacks; at the Sandhurst Public Library we had rickety shelves.

Promise wanted us to meet there, in the stacks, and bring our lips together, stealing kisses not so much from each other, or even the librarian, as from the books surrounding us on all sides. And sitting now at the table, considering this proposal, I was thinking of those huge jugs of pennies at the county fair—you'd win a prize for guessing their number. How many kisses were there amid the modest holdings of the Sandhurst Public Library? How long would it take us to make up the difference? I didn't know about Promise, but for me kissing had become a craving—like the urge to pick at a scab or reach again, deeper into the same cookie jar.

And so we got up and went to the H-P aisle.

— —

Where have you been?

Library, I said.

All day?

What are we watching? I asked—sitting down and realizing again the difficulty of viewing television through a network of tipped squares. Even at this late date, it took some getting used to. But it would've been cruel to put the television on my side of the fence. With or without handcuffs, Bob was bearing the brunt of the scenario I'd mustered; and the television was important to Bob, if only because of the possibility of seeing dispatches about himself. Apparently the books, sitting on the shelf I'd built above the refrigerator, were stale news.

It's a special report on prisons in America, he said. Ted Koppel's inside a prison.

Hard to imagine Ted Koppel in a prison.

No need to imagine, Bob said—directing my eyes to the screen with a lift of his chin.

I stared at the television and saw Koppel sitting on one side of a bare table made of shiny steel. He looked somehow incongruous. Dressed casually, his plaid shirt open at the collar, he could easily have wandered over to chat up the common folk at the next picnic table. Across from him, in an orange short-sleeved jumpsuit, sat an inmate with biceps the size of bread loaves.

Is that where I'm going to end up? I asked.

That guy there in the orange with the tattoos, Bob said, he's your next boyfriend.

No. I believe that's your department.

— —

And so we got up and went to the H-P aisle. No one else was there, of course. In the middle of the day, before school had been let out, the library was almost empty. Without any discussion, we kissed without hands. She held hers behind her back—for safekeeping. I thought once or twice of touching Promise's oval-shaped face, or placing a hand at the back of her head, with the idea of a slight insistence. But it was better without hands. Lips, mouths, tongues. My eyes closed, I could see nothing at all. I was swimming in the dark, in warm water—like an adolescent in the summertime at Poygan Lake, past the midnight curfew. Our tongues were synchronized swimmers, I couldn't help thinking—a bad analogy that I would never have used in writing, and yet here it was, zooming through my mind, and doing nothing to lessen the pleasure.

Kissing—it can make you very silly in the head.

— —

Come on. Show me. Show me the novel.

Why?

I mean, what the hell? Bob said—shrugging. God knows I've

got a little time on my hands, so why not? Hand it over. Let me see the beast.

The beast? I sat there on my side of the fence and stared. Did he know what he was saying? Maybe the two cups of coffee I'd already brought him had loosened him up. Or was this the new, exuberant Bob—a man whose spirits were rising as his weight went down? Or was he just getting tired of counting the days and crossing his fingers and showing off a restraint he thought might catapult me toward kindness.

How much do you think there is? I asked him.

Many of our best writers aren't prolific.

Joyce Carol Oates?

Not one of our best writers, in my opinion. I know her editor. She feeds a certain threshold market in the literary genre. That's my personal opinion.

What's my market? I said, and at that moment I was thinking only of Food Town a mile away, where I'd gone for groceries the night before and brought home more of the raspberries he couldn't get enough of. In a better world, Lloyd might've dropped them, one by one, into Bob's open mouth.

You said you had sixteen notebooks, he said. That's more than a little.

I stared at Bob and thought of the thin green notebooks—the most recent ones—stacked on the corner of a shelf in the kitchen. I've stopped that, I said.

Stopped what? he said. Writing in the notebooks?

No, the novel. I've stopped that novel.

Why? The one about the man who couldn't get the elusive woman in the white shirt and so settled for the other woman? You stopped that one?

Yeah. That one. It's kaput.

I wondered, was that what my novel had been about? Did Bob's words fairly describe the work I'd done—that is, did they capture my vain attempt to tell a story? *The one about the man who couldn't get the elusive woman in the white shirt and so settled for the other woman.* I couldn't really blame Bob for his pat summary. (Although I did worry: Would he have made the same dismissive comment about my newest effort? *The one about the man who couldn't get published and so kidnapped the editor.*) I should never have read him that passage—about the woman in the white shirt; and now my stupid mistake was coming back to haunt me even more than the memory of the stillborn novel's page-by-page meanderings. *Kaput.*

Bob and I sat in an uncomfortable silence—a perfectly reasonable response to death, I thought. What was there to say, after all? Maybe that novel, like its predecessors, never had a heartbeat in the first place. Maybe it was only an imaginary novel. Maybe I was destined to act out the part of the crazy woman who finds out, yet again, that her pregnancy was hysterical.

What's my market? I finally said, returning to the earlier question.

The *market,* Bob said—speaking the solemn word, looking up, ostensibly for inspiration.

— —

At the library, Promise and I sat at our table and spoke in muted tones—first about her dog, Hans, and his persistently wet, drippy nose and what *that* might suggest in the way of illness, and then about a strange gentleman in the corner, wearing a herringbone coat and noisily licking his finger before turning each page of *Fortune.* We talked until the librarian looked over, raised her bushy red eyebrows, and crossed the line of her almost-nonexistent lips with a finger. I don't know about Promise, but this *shushing* struck me as slightly unfair. On a regular basis, pretty much every afternoon, children ran, chortled, screamed, sometimes even heaved and vomited—and so how exactly were *we* disturbing the peace? I'd come to the conclusion that Ms. Prissy, the head librarian, was not happy with the way we enjoyed our days while she stood in rubber-soled shoes behind the counter of a library barely worthy of the name.

A moment later, Promise notified me—in written form, on a

page torn from her wire-bound journal and pushed silently across the table to one side of my open briefcase—that she'd dreamed about me. *Last night I had a dream about Evan Ulmer.* There was, below this declaration, a tiny, adroit drawing of a sleeping stick figure and a coil of *z*'s escaping upward; and then, below that, a brief account of the dream.

Before delving into the dream itself, I glanced up from the piece of paper and looked at Promise. She was staring right at me, her eyes big and wide, pursing her lips as though she were kissing her image in a mirror.

And what did it feel like—this revelation, this notification of having entered her mind in the depths of the wee hours, under cover of dream?

— —

Before, I said to Bob, were you happy?

Before what?

Before I abducted you.

Nineteen days ago, coming back from lunch? At that particular moment? On that particular day?

Not just that day. In general. Say you considered me a very close friend and I asked, and you were giving me the straight scoop, what would you tell me? *Yes, I am, I'm very happy. Thanks for asking.*

Happy? Maybe. Very happy? I don't think so.

Why not? I asked—clearing my throat.

I'm just not a *very* person. I don't think I've ever been *very* anything. Certainly not happy.

Very successful?

As an editor? he said. Maybe. Depending on your criteria. No one has ever asked me to be editor in chief.

Bob and I stared at each other through the fence. I noticed, as I hadn't before, that Bob's mouth made a perfect horizontal line across his face. In time, as he got older, would the edges descend, like in a cartoon of unhappiness?

What would need to happen in your life, I asked, to make you very happy?

Why are you asking?

Just tell me.

Right now? Bob said—and he turned to look behind him, at the Porta-Potty and the IKEA bunk bed that had somehow soothed his chronic back problem. Well, I might be happier if—

No, no, I said—cutting him off, holding a hand up and squeezing my eyes shut. If I let you go, would that really change anything?

That wasn't what I—

What if you had a skirmish with death or danger or whatever you want to call it? And then you escaped. And then you realized just how very, very happy you really were. That sometimes happens, doesn't it?

I don't know what you're talking about, he said.

People survive plane crashes, I said, and their lives are forever changed. They've been yelling at their wives, or they've been mean to the gardener, and suddenly all that goes away. Suddenly they have a new lease on life. You know what I mean?

Yeah, OK, Bob said—nodding. That could happen, it's certainly possible.

I don't think so, I said—slowly shaking my head. I can't see that happening in your case. You'd be well rested, especially the way you've been sleeping lately. And you'd be in better shape, certainly. So maybe I've done you a service, brought you to a place in your life, a kind of plateau—

Thanks.

And now you can stay there and not let yourself slip again. But I don't think so. Sooner or later I'll let you go and you'll just get heavy again—

Heavy?

And you'll make a few authors very happy. You'll kiss the cheeks of a few important agents, and that'll be that. And what good is that?

None, Bob said. You might as well just let me go now.

No, not just yet, I said—shaking my head.

Did you ever torture animals as a child?

How do you mean? I said. Put cats in the freezer for a few hours? Swing 'em around by their tails? Stick firecrackers up their asses and light them? No, that wasn't me. You're thinking of the *other* kids. I got involved in animal rights and handed out leaflets about the immorality of fur at the Valley Fair Mall. God's creatures and the sanctity of the earth and all that. That was the kind of kid I was. What kind were you?

I never handed out leaflets, Bob said, but I was pretty much the same. Minus the religious angle.

You know what I think?

What?

I think you'd have done exactly the same thing if you were in my shoes. I think if you'd struggled like I've struggled—

Everyone struggles, Evan.

If everyone struggles and almost no one abducts editors at major publishing houses, then what would you say is wrong with me and how would you account for this? I said—sweeping a hand above my head like a lasso, to indicate the chain-link fence, the Porta-Potty, the treadmill, the soundproofing, the bunk beds, the whole universe conjured up in an otherwise unassuming basement in a house in a hamlet outside of New York, New York.

Don't be so dramatic, Bob said. Maybe you just needed a friend.

So I'm a lonely fuck.

I didn't say that.

I *am* a lonely fuck, Bob. That's pretty obvious. But if I wanted a friend, I could've gotten a therapist. They don't require as much upkeep. And anyway I have a friend. A *new* friend.

Yes. You met her at the library.

I did? I said—clearing my throat.

I assume you did.

Is it that obvious? Or is this one of your educated guesses?

Excuse me for asking, Bob said, but what's the thing with the throat clearing?

— —

And what did it feel like—this revelation, this notification of having entered her mind in the depths of the wee hours, under cover of dream? A woman's mind, *her* mind.

Sitting across from Promise, I chose not to reveal how happy it made me, if only because I could see, out of the corner of my eye, the librarian still watching us. But looking down at that piece of paper, at Promise's longhand and her first sentence—*Last night I had a dream about Evan Ulmer*—I thought about how jubilant I always felt to know that I'd been in someone else's dream. That I was on someone's, if not everyone's, mind—it was very sweet.

Moving on to the content of the dream, I read the words: *You were dressed up as a gorilla, visiting New York, where I was living. I asked how you were. I just wanted to know how you were. The way people politely ask people every day. "And how are you today?" But you wouldn't answer. You just kept doing the gorilla imitation. And I kept asking and then I got angry, and you still wouldn't answer my stupid question. You know, because gorillas can't talk. That was your point and you were stubborn in holding to it.*

There was something girlish about Promise's penmanship—not cloudlike circles above her *i*'s, but a certain loopiness that gave away her gender. Or was it her age? Of course I'd stared at her words before, guessing at their meaning from across the table; but that had been a fruitless, upside-down exercise. This was new information. Was it a cruel antidote, to the good feeling of having appeared in her dream, that got me thinking of Promise as dangerously unknowable? I was a gorilla, through and through, destined never to speak a word. But what about Promise and *her* future? Who might she become?

— —

Excuse me for asking, Bob said, but what's the thing with the throat clearing?

Right then and there—having been alerted to the possibility, the idea of it—I felt the tickle in the back of my throat, the same one that always prompted the tightening of my esophagus and the thick, deep swallow that produced only a small satisfaction. *A Leroy in your throat*, my mother used to call it, harking back to the name of my favorite stuffed animal—a frog as green as grass, as big as the length of a little boy's arm. But I wasn't a child when I first felt the tickle, now was I?

That? I said—clearing my throat. Each time there was a wonderful illusion that it would be the last time, the end of something—like a shoe lowering itself on the hunched back of a crunchy spider. It's just something that gets caught in my throat.

It's like a tic, Bob said.

It bothers you, right?

No, I'm just curious. I used to chew my nails.

I watched Bob as he fanned his ten fingers out in front of him, the ordinariness of these nails supposedly harboring a backstory about old compulsions. But I was having a difficult time believing him. Had there really ever been something that made him choose, day in and day out, between giving in or denying himself the pleasure? Had he, for example, ever really felt the sheer terror of writing?

6

*My novel falls under the rubric of what the fawning host refers
to as* extraordinary; *and yet again and again (the camera rolling) I come off as too thankful for the turn of fate that allowed
me to publish a novel after years and years of dry, humiliat-
ing silence. Pressed to explain the book, I either come up short
or ramble incoherently. And anyway, isn't it tedious—having
to take success and turn it into a tale of perseverance, giving
testimony to a public trustful of the publishing industry as just
arbiter in a world of words spilled like seed everywhere you step?
Even fantasy success gets snatched away from you and shaped
into a story to inspire others, to offer hope to the hopeless—losers,
every one of them, for seeing their fate changing, and just in the
nick of time.*

*Sitting there across from the host, I push on and finally ar-
rive at a way of making sense of my work. To explain my novel
about a man who abducts another man and keeps him in his
basement, I talk about the impetus to write:* I'd fallen into a
hole, it seemed. And, gnawing on my own hand, I couldn't
help but think of writing as a weapon. My next novel, I
told myself—it was going to be an assault on the publishing world. I'd dare them to publish it. They'd resist, of
course. Eventually, though, the book would be published.
And in having written the novel, and in standing up to a
weary but powerful industry, I'd be making a bold statement. It wasn't only my perseverance that readers would
admire but my gumption in exploring the subtle horrors of
living among the wannabe riffraff. The plot would involve
the stuff of nightly television news and weekly magazines.
I might even end up on television myself, something of a
sudden star.

A LMOST A MONTH into the abduction scenario I found myself trying to remember what it had been like before. My life—what had it been like? Before I'd seen Robert Partnow's picture in *Publishers Weekly,* before I bought the gun, soundproofed the basement, secured the Porta-Potty. Before I visited the Evergreen Building, did the deed, got into a writing groove, fell into the habit of sitting slack-jawed with Bob and watching one *Dateline, 20-20, 60 Minutes, 48 Hours, Prime Time* "special" after another. Before trips to the library and meeting Promise and weird conversations, strange feelings, and the pastime of kissing. What had life been like back then, before? And suddenly *before* seemed very long ago. It was as though my life had been sliced into halves and now—in the tumult of the second half—it was high time to reconsider the first half. Of course the division made no sense: three and a half weeks not the same as forty years. But that's what it felt like—the present choking the past even more than usual.

Above all else, I felt relieved. It was like that *now-let's-take-a-deep-breath-and-let-it-out* relief I'd sometimes feel at the end of a difficult day—anxiety miraculously lifting as the lids of my eyes descended. Nighttime now, shades drawn, and I hadn't *lost it,* whatever there was to lose. I hadn't reached across the counter at Macy's and throttled the rude employee, I hadn't absentmindedly reached down the kitchen drain with the garbage disposal on. I hadn't made *the mistake of a lifetime.* It was like waking up from a nightmare: your head was groggy, but at least you hadn't stabbed your boss in the heart with his favorite Montblanc.

I'd abducted a semi-famous editor and now we were discussing, in an increasingly civil tone, the pulse of the nation and the reasons for our limited happiness. I had a girlfriend, or at least I was brushing my teeth more often. Changes had occurred. The floodgates had opened and no one had drowned. All limbs intact, the mind still crawling its way through a maze of thought. *And* I was writing.

Caring for Bob, doing errands, working on my new manuscript about an abduction, seeing Promise—day after day I felt somehow, for the first time, reconciled with the world. I was a new man, the man I'd always been meaning to be. (The only one I could ever hope to be?) I'm exaggerating, of course. But it *did* feel new and different. I was almost happy.

— • —

I've ended up watching too much television, Bob said.

I've noticed that.

And sometimes these reports—

The ones about *you,* I said.

Yes, the ones about me. They depress me.

I didn't want to push too hard—after all, we were building a fledgling intimacy—but I wondered if what really depressed Bob was the relative *absence* of such reports over the last few days. Almost a month into the abduction scenario, the weekly TV news "magazines" and the gossip shows had clearly grown weary of the story—the trail going cold, the homosexual angle losing its edge.

Hey, I hear Lloyd's business is booming, I said to Bob. I didn't tell you but there was a little thing in the *Observer* last week about it. Just a couple paragraphs. Some nonsense about grief and flowers and business and the power of media exposure.

Bob looked at me, and I couldn't make out his expression. Was he suspicious of me? Did he think I might be making up this story about Lloyd? Had I already thrown the issue out, or was it still in the stack in the kitchen?

Between you and me, Evan—

And then he hesitated, as sometimes happens with this prefatory phrase, this nod to the conspiratorial. *Between you and me.* And I had to love that hesitation, what it told me about who I'd become.

Yes—

I think he's been milking the celebrity factor.

Lloyd, I said.

Yes.

And that disturbs you.

It does, Bob said. At least a little. But it's not really that. It just confirms certain things.

What things?

I don't blame him, he said—looking away from me. It's been like this for a while, and it's nobody's fault.

I could see that Bob wouldn't continue without me, wouldn't go further without the prodding of my questions. And for a second I felt like the hamster who discovers that the food pellets come only when you push your nose against the bar.

Like what? I said. It's been like what for a while?

It's lost something, he said.

It's lost—

I don't know. Excitement? You know, first it's nothing, then it's a relationship, and then it's an idea or a memory. Excitement doesn't last forever, does it? Everyone has to grow up, face reality once in a while. Except maybe you, Evan. That's probably why you write.

How do you mean?

Doesn't it do that? Bob said—staring over at the stack of books, the untouched library. From a writer's point of view, doesn't writing create excitement? Doesn't it *re*create it?

— ▬ —

On the front porch, Promise and I kissed hello. It was a short kiss, the kind I might've exchanged with my mother—which was fine. We were expanding our repertoire, I told myself. And then she introduced me to Hans, her ten-year-old with a runny nose. The dog, a black mutt who had the girth of a bulldog and the abbreviated tail of a pointer, circled me in a kind of frenzy. I didn't say so to Promise, but he looked like a little pig.

Inside, Promise swung her arm to indicate the expanse of the house. And it *was* a large house, much bigger than mine. The furniture didn't seem special, but then this was obviously a second house—a vacation home, a refuge from the daily travails of Manhattan. It was a sprawling, two-story structure in a serene setting, and that was enough. And wouldn't any sort of furniture have paled in comparison to whatever might've graced the Buckleys' lovely Upper East Side apartment?

Barefoot, Promise had her hair held up on both sides by purple clips I'd never seen before. She offered me a choice of beverages—a Coke, a glass of orange juice, a Bloody Mary. I didn't know whether that last offering was a joke or not. She seemed suddenly inscrutable, as though being in her own house had given her new powers.

When she left the room, Hans—hunkered down with head on paws—stared at me from his perch at the top of the stairs. What could *he* have been thinking? Downstairs, I looked at small photographs of summer outings hung in clusters of thin gold frames on the walls. A stuffed teddy bear, missing an ear, lay abandoned on a wooden rocking chair that had seen better days. Bookshelves, large and small, covered whatever wall space wasn't taken up with photographs; the books were piled sideways, one on top of the other.

I stared at the books, their publishers' insignia, and thought of Bob, who was probably an invisible presence behind a few of these titles. Did he miss his responsibilities at work? Not for the first time, I imagined Bob trying to escape in my absence. It was now becoming a sort of foregone conclusion, Bob's departure. Sooner or later it would happen—eventuality held the trump card, as always. But what would follow Bob's release? That was the real question. It was *my* question, obviously, and yet I heard it like a narrator's interrogative in one of my green notebooks—egging me on.

Waiting for Promise, I thought of my father and what he would make of this house, this sabbatical milieu, this young woman gone to the kitchen in her bare feet. There wasn't much to wonder—not really; she was obviously a young woman who would know when to say good-bye, when to send Evan away, shut the door, and turn off the light. But, more to the point, what would my father think of Bob and the status of the abduction scenario? That it was another sign of his son's life tipping to slosh its dashed hopes? I could easily imagine him—eyes closed, head shaking in slow motion in a kind of fatherly incredulity.

I almost jumped out of my skin when Promise suddenly appeared—a can of Coke in each hand.

— —

For a while there, you know, I was farther along than the others.

What others?

My contemporaries, I said—sitting on the first step on the stairs, barely in view of Bob, up on his treadmill. I've been complimented on my writing skills since I was a child.

Back there in Appleton, Bob said—nodding.

Birthplace of Henry Houdini.

I didn't know that.

World headquarters of the John Birch Society. Our dual claim to glory.

Scary, he said.

After forty minutes of walking and then jogging, Bob had worked himself into a thick sweat, the back of his yellow T-shirt now a Rorschach test. It looked to me like two dogs in a tussle.

In graduate school, I said, I published a story before anyone else had even gotten bold enough to submit one.

Published where?

A stupid little journal, Bob. It doesn't matter. And these little successes, these compliments can go to your head, and then later they just slip into the past like distant memories. Like Santa Claus, the chimney, the Easter bunny, the tooth fairy. Like some car that keeps revving its engine but never fucking *moves*.

Nice image, Bob said—head nodding, legs pumping. Caught at the stoplight. Car idling with menace. I like it.

You like it? You *like* it?

Bob stopped the treadmill, got off, used a hand to work a blue cotton towel around his neck. He bent over, hands on his knees, and I could see his pink scalp—it was the shade of a dog's underbelly. When he looked up, he let me know with a simple flash of his eyes that—yes, he knew. He knew I was annoyed. And, as silly as it sounds, it made all the difference.

———

I almost jumped out of my skin when Promise suddenly appeared—a can of Coke in each hand. Hans bounded down the stairs, his little rear end moving back and forth in lieu of a tail. Promise handed me one of the red cans. She was wearing a blue T-shirt that had the words COLD BLISTER scrawled in black cursive across the front. Was this a band?

Why do you stack the books that way? I asked—pointing to one of the shelves.

That's my father. He has a bad neck—and Promise twisted hers sideways, ear to shoulder, to demonstrate how a person normally looks at books.

So many, I said—clearing my throat, swallowing hard. A lawyer interested in books?

You should see the apartment in New York. More nonfiction than fiction. Lots of American history. But yes, he's a reader. Definitely.

And your mother?

She's illiterate.

She's not, I said.

OK, she's not, Promise said. But almost. And a self-described museum slut. What about your parents?

They're dead.

I *know* that.

They weren't readers when they were alive. Well, that's not entirely true. My mother read detective novels. She devoured them like candy.

There are worse addictions.

Science fiction?

Cigarettes, she said—and then I could see she regretted having said it.

That afternoon, sitting in the house, we talked mostly about Promise. We talked about her childhood, a skiing accident when she was six, her senior thesis on Emily Dickinson, the subsequent year in Paris on a Fulbright, and what she called her *forlorn temperament,* which persisted despite academic success and parents who loved each other. It was that *inability to get along with others,* she said, harking back to a comment scribbled by a Mrs. Wagner on a first-grade report card. Making friends sometimes seemed like a chore.

I found this a little hard to believe, seeing as how she'd singled me out. And I didn't say so, but I was wondering whether Promise was in a phase. Wouldn't she soon come to see me as a momentary curiosity, a mistake of personal hygiene? Give her a year, and wouldn't she be living again in Manhattan, awash in friends, leading the kind of life I'd always wanted to lead?

Promise had withdrawn to Sandhurst and shut herself up in this house to set about meeting a new challenge: she would become a writer, produce a novel or a collection of stories. It was a house that held childhood memories—she'd mostly stopped coming in her teenage years, she said. Other than a few boring neighbors, she knew no one in Sandhurst. No one except for *Evan Ulmer.* She sometimes said my name, spoke of me in the third person.

He's a curious man, she said—as we sipped Coke. I'm thinking of writing something about a character based on Evan Ulmer.

I smiled and nodded. And considered whether I was wrong about Promise. Maybe it wasn't a phase at all.

— —

Had you been there before? Bob asked.

To her house? No. First time.

And you were there for—

For? You mean why I was there, my—

No.

My purpose?

No, he said. How *long* were you there? For how long?

Two hours, I said.

And so did you—

We kissed, I said, and a little more. But no, if you mean *that*.

I didn't mean *that*. I don't particularly believe in *that*.

What does that mean? I said.

What does *what* mean?

You said you didn't believe—

I'm talking about intimacies, Bob said. You know, about *fucking*. I've got nothing against it. It's just I don't think it counts above everything else. I think of pleasure more as being on a spectrum. Don't you?

— —

Of course I was never any good at it. Usually it was that I just couldn't keep my mouth shut. I tried to keep things from Promise, sometimes for her own good. It didn't help that she asked me so many questions—a habit of hers, at least in relation to me. Things were gaining momentum, and our bodies were only part of it. There was me, a ball of string; there was Promise, a curious cat; and so, of course, things were unraveling in unpredictable ways. I tried to keep quiet about the yapping dog, my disappointment in myself, my recent case of hemorrhoids, the money my parents left me—but then I ended up telling her anyway. (Loyalty to Hans didn't keep her from saying she absolutely hated chihuahuas.) One little secret got shooed out the door, and just as quickly another would take its place in the queue—some piece of myself, retrieved from my stash of self-incriminations. I waited for Promise to disapprove, but she never did. In fact she almost seemed calmed by my shameful tales. She'd look at me, smile, frown, and earnestly bob her head at the latest revelation.

I'd let loose these little parts of myself, and she'd sit there nodding, and sometimes I'd wonder whether she was there at all—whether, in some strange sense, I was talking to myself. I was addressing those blue eyes of hers, but maybe I was really cajoling myself—holding out the carrot of hope, trying to convince myself of my honesty and integrity. And I kept feeling that I hadn't yet revealed things, not really. Not the kinds of things that would determine whether or not I was only a momentary curiosity. There was still an important side of myself I hadn't shared with Promise.

But then how was I to talk about Bob? What would she think of *that,* what would she make of me after I'd lifted the velvet rope between fiction and reality? She obviously believed in the blurring of that line, in the way autobiographical details can feed the imagination; but that didn't mean she'd honor a total breakdown of the distinction. Telling her about Bob was like telling her, *Oh, by the way, every other Tuesday afternoon I molest children from the neighborhood in my basement.*

Who knows, maybe I was wrong. By summertime, could it be— Promise and Bob shaking pinkies through the chain-link fence, chatting nostalgically about life back in big, bad Manhattan?

— —

Come on, Evan. Why not? I tell you things.

I tell you plenty.

But you don't *show* me anything, Bob said.

It's rough, I said.

So there *is* something. Something new?

Yes, I said—the word escaping my mouth like an envelope dropped in a mailbox. No turning back now.

What's it about?

It's new, I said. I'm working on something new.

Good. So let me have a look-see.

I haven't yet rescued it from its genre, I said. It's too much a reworking of—

Everything's a reworking of something, Evan.

You wouldn't like it.

Maybe I wouldn't, he said. But then maybe I would.

— —

Why Kafka?

I'd asked Promise that question more than once. I told her I was ignorant of Kafka's fiction and autobiographical scribblings. I'd read him, of course—who hadn't, at one time or another? But what did I remember? At best, fuzzy fragments—insects, bureaucratic corridors, hungry artists, labyrinthine castles, deficient fathers. In his personal life, Kafka had had troubles with women and never managed to leap across the abyss into marriage. I'd picked that up from somewhere and remembered it, perhaps because of my own difficulties. Beyond that I knew nothing—not until I picked up *The Castle* at Rizzoli's on an excursion to Manhattan. (I felt guilty in not buying it from Sandhurst's own meager Booknook, where I'd browsed in spite of Promise's prideful claim that she'd avoided the store since her fifteenth birthday.) I bought Kafka's novel in honor of Promise. I began to read it on the Metro-North back to Sandhurst, and immediately I fell prey to the novel's paranoia, its voice—quietly obsessive. It was like sugar poured directly from box into open mouth.

—·—

Here's how I imagined it. My father was strapped to a chair, the sports page—a sort of daily reward—dangling from a string to entice him into plowing through the words written by his son. How could I tell he was actually reading? Small wires were attached to his brain, inserted with sharp and slender needles, and hooked up at the other end a lightbulb that went on and off after each sentence read. And the pages of the book were turned, with some fanfare, by Vanna White. (This was a nod toward my father's favorite wet dream.) And so on, until he'd read the whole book—mouth covered with duct tape, nostrils flaring in a futile effort to escape.

Like in *A Clockwork Orange,* Bob said.

I had popped down to the basement and mentioned my little fantasy, leaving out the part about Vanna White.

What about it? I said. What about *A Clockwork Orange?*

Did you see the movie?

A long time ago.

A guy is forced to watch a movie. His eyeballs are held open for hours. He's strapped to a chair.

So what are you saying, Bob? That that's where I got the idea?

I'm not saying anything.

Yes you are, I said.

No, I'm not.

Everyone is always saying something, I thought—looking at Bob, clearing my throat, keeping my own counsel. Even people with their mouths taped shut. Even in your fantasies, the parade of rebukes never stops.

—‐

Is it a—

I waited for Promise to finish her question. We were standing outside the library, next to the bicycle racks. But her words hung there in the air between us, and her eyes looked into my eyes. Individually, one at a time. And with her eyes doing this darting, she fell toward me, as though losing her balance, and kissed me.

Is it a what? I said—once our mouths disengaged. My lips were getting a little chapped; I'd noticed this that morning while shaving.

A problem. Is it a problem?

Is what a problem? I said—feeling a catch in my throat, not quite enough to warrant clearing it. How do you define *problem*?

A problem is when it's not enough.

You like to go slow, I said.

I *love* to go slow.

Yes, I know. I mean, I noticed.

And so that's a problem.

It's *not* a problem, I said.

And you'd tell me?

I tell you far too much already.

But you would? she asked. You'd tell me?

It makes you anxious, I said—and it surprised me, even as I said it.

Yes, of course, Promise said—and her eyes, as though under the influence of a truth serum, kept darting. And with my face so close to hers, I found my eyes doing the same, moving from blue eye to blue eye and then back. It made me dizzy.

Have you ever been with an older woman?

Older? I said. You mean—

Fifty, say.

No. Why?

Just wondering, Promise said.

— —

Halfway down the stairs, I could already hear Oprah. In spite of the calm resonance of her voice, she always seemed to be bellowing, barking, bringing a sort of heft to the proceedings. Bob was watching intently. He didn't look over at me, even though I knew he'd heard my steps on the stairs. I could've taken this badly, but lately Bob and I had been getting along, finding our speed; and somehow he seemed newly capable of acknowledging me without any overt sign.

Any requests for dinner?

Whatever, Bob said.

What are the girls talking about today? I asked—approaching the chain-link fence.

It's not all girls. Check out the guy at the end there.

He's the ringleader, I said. He's the safe cock, the limp dick. The girls love him. They worship him.

You're in an *up* mood, Bob said.

He's wearing a sweater vest, I said. That's a dead giveaway. What more needs to be said?

He has an advanced degree in family counseling.

Of course he does.

We like to refer to these as lightbulb moments, Oprah was saying.

That moment when everything becomes clear. Something clicks, a light goes on, and life never looks the same. You know you've discovered something important—something that resonates so completely, it can change your life. And once a lightbulb comes on, it's up to you to use that light. Take the example of Sharon Tisdale, a young woman overwhelmed and suicidal. During an unexpected stop in the middle of a busy highway, she had a moment of clarity that changed the way she looked at herself and gave her the strength to choose life.

I'll change the channel, Bob said. It's just a rerun.

No, don't, I said. The self-help impulse, isn't that right up your alley?

Leaning into the fence and gripping it with my hands, I was reminded of watching Little League games as a kid. What with the danger of foul balls smashing fingers, there had been a prohibition on gripping the fence. Now, here—perhaps experiencing my own *lightbulb moment*—I felt as though I was getting away with something.

I'm leaving anyway, I said.

Library?

On the screen, the woman with dirty-blonde hair said something—words coming murkily through her tears—as another woman pressed a consoling hand on the puffy sleeve of her flowered dress. The guy in the sweater vest leaned forward, as though to listen more intently.

They're getting in touch, I said. They're laying their cards out on the table. Look at the women in the audience, they're nodding their heads yes, yes, yes. *I was in that exact situation just a couple of years ago. I know what you're talking about. I've cried those same tears.*

Bob switched the television off and turned to me—the remote a weapon of obliteration, the blank screen now a provocation.

Does anyone ever know what we're talking about? I asked.

What are we talking about?

Does anyone care? I said—and instantly I felt the pathos of that question, as though Oprah had tiptoed her way into my soul. And it

came to me that there were people—Claudia, the daughters Bob refused to speak of, authors like adopted children, even Lloyd—who
cared more than I might imagine, even if they couldn't begin to
know what it was really like here at our little place in Sandhurst.

I'm sorry, I said—and I didn't wait for Bob to ask why. Had he
seen? Had he sensed the tears welling up? Up the stairs I went like a
shot, the Sandhurst Public Library my destination and refuge.

7

◄○►

What was it? Maybe it was the steady diet of Westerns, encouraged by older parents beholden to another era. As a boy, growing up in Appleton, Wisconsin, glued to the television set, I didn't think revenge was such a bad word. Sometimes you had to take matters into your own hands. It always brought to mind the image of a stoic on horseback, giving up the ease of domestic life, wandering through shitty little towns in search of the one responsible for the death of Luke, a treasured cowhand. Usually there was a moment of confrontation—finding the offender, pulling the trigger, taking revenge. But I never found myself interested in that moment. Instead I was always drawn to the wandering, the searching, the scheming, the way a life gets seized, taken over, all of a sudden dedicated to revenge. No different than a life given over to the pursuit of happiness or wealth or fame. And isn't that one way of defining revenge—ambition by other means?

So you know robert partnow?
Robert—

That editor, the one who disappeared, Promise said—and in the background, over the phone, I could hear a newspaper rustling. You know, the one who got kidnapped. Abducted. Whatever.

Yes, I remember, I said. I heard about it. Read it in the paper.

I wondered if that was behind your story, Evan. The one about the kidnapping. Was this Partnow thing a kind of inspiration?

How do they know it's an abduction?

The papers say that, Promise said. And according to my mother, that's what people are saying. My uncle actually knows this Partnow guy. So that story *didn't* inspire your story?

No. I began it about a year ago, I just couldn't get anywhere with it. And so I recently—

I thought it was *new,* Promise said—and I could almost see the symmetrical, quizzical dip of agile eyebrows.

So what else does your uncle say? I asked.

My uncle? He just went to college with him, he doesn't really know him. But he's supposed to be a nice guy, actually.

Partnow.

Yeah, and they think it's a disgruntled author, maybe someone dropped from the—

From the—

What's it called? she said—and in the background I could hear her fingers snapping. The *midlist.* Isn't that what it's called? Probably some author dropped from the midlist. That's what my mother told me, though you've got to take *that* into account. The source. My mother. Not exactly the horse's mouth. Hey, guess what? She's coming for a visit.

Your mother? Here?

Where else? Promise said. In a week. Want to meet her?

Sure.

— ◦ —

I looked around the basement and had a sudden fright in not seeing Bob. But there he was—coming out of the Porta-Potty. As soon as he got his pants zipped up, I asked the question that Promise had inserted into the loop of my mind.

Is this a question about me? he said—skirting my question. Or about the news media and their need to tell stories regardless of the truth?

I'm just wondering, I said—clearing my throat, looking over toward the bed, where Bob kept his stash of news clippings, his little heap of *Bob* speculation.

According to what *I've* read, I'm a happy man who had no reason to up and leave.

I mean, doesn't it bother you, Bob? Why does everyone just *assume* you've been abducted? Couldn't you just as easily have skipped town, decided to change your life? And I hate to say it, but it's always the same old story. Robert Partnow, pencil-pushing editor, father of two, married for sixteen years to the wonderful and long-suffering Claudia. Abducted by a pissed-off author with some serious mental problems. Both of us, we're being slighted in the public imagination.

Both of us—

I don't mean our situations are comparable—

Evan, have you ever thought of *not* feeling sorry for yourself?

I looked at Bob, a little shocked. But I held my tongue; I was trying to stay mindful of Bob's situation—stuck in Sandhurst, overdosed on television, losing weight but also, along with it, a measure of dignity. How easy could that be?

Did you ever see that old movie *The Passenger*?

No.

Directed by Antonioni, I said. Jack Nicholson purposely disappears, takes on a dead man's identity, changes his life, meets Maria Schneider. Why doesn't someone speculate about that? One man dies, another is given new life. Maybe if I die—

There's a thought.

Seriously, Bob, imagine it. I die. You take the gun and shoot me. The gun?

I die and then you could become me.

Evan Ulmer, Bob said—saying it fast, giving my name the sound of a new strain of bacteria. Thanks, Evan, but I think I'll pass.

— —

At the library, a boy wet his pants and the urine dripped onto to the linoleum floor under his chair. Promise and I watched the whole thing from across the way—our notebooks open, pens poised. The librarian reacted with remarkable grace. She and her colleagues may have been inept at keeping periodicals up to date, but they knew how to deal with life's little lapses. If it had been me, I would've pointed the boy's mother toward the restroom where she'd find ready means for cleaning up the mess herself.

Reminds me of the time I had a little accident at the opera, Promise said—looking at me with narrowed eyes, almost as though she couldn't quite believe what she was about to say. Placido Domingo was going full throttle on *Turandot,* and I was in utter misery. My poor little bladder.

Little girls weren't meant for the opera, I said.

Not when it's Puccini at three hours.

Together Promise and I watched as the boy's mother tried to dry the bottoms of his tiny sneakers with a newspaper taken from her purse. He was crying silently. He was frowning so hard it looked as though his forehead was going to split in two.

What would Kafka say? I asked—repeating a question that had quickly become an interrogatory staple, a game Promise and I were playing more and more often.

Franz? Franz was adverse to all bodily functions. The body was a torment, even before the tuberculosis. He was embarrassed by his body.

Will the boy remember this incident? I asked. As a forty-year-old man, will he think back to that awful, embarrassing day in the Sandhurst library?

I remember the opera.

You're twenty-five, I said, not forty.

And in that moment—as we watched the librarian wield the mop, the boy's mother wiping tears from his eyes with the sleeve of her blouse—I imagined Promise at forty. What would become of her? Would she, by that date, have achieved a level of literary success? Would a bit of gray have found its way into her skirt of hair? Would she have found a man like her father with whom she could spend the rest of her life? More to the point, would she remember Evan Ulmer?

— —

When did you write this? Bob said—holding the manuscript in his lap, squeezing it until he had it bowed into a makeshift telescope.

Does it matter?

It's just I'm surprised, he said.

Why?

Well, it's very good. It is. It really is. But—

And that surprises you?

What surprises me is I hadn't expected to be reading about myself, Bob said—sliding his reading glasses down and using two hands in unison to flip the pages until he came upon the passage he was looking for. *Despite the thinning hair at the front of his head and the goofy smile, he wasn't such a bad-looking fellow. Slightly overweight, maybe. He was like a dark-haired cross between John Malkovich and Kelsey Grammer.*

How do you know I'm writing about you?

My name's Bob.

News flash, I said—my right hand a prop, a flashbulb exploding.
You're not the only Bob in the world. It's a common name.

He lowered his chin and stared at me over his glasses—a gesture
of incredulity that, for once, made him look like a genuine homosexual. His brow furrowed. Then he looked back down, flipped a
couple of pages. *I was trying to stay mindful of Bob's situation—stuck
in Sandhurst, overdosed on television, losing weight but also, along with
it, a measure of dignity. How easy could that be?*

You hadn't expected—

I hadn't expected to be reading about myself, Evan. That's what
I'm saying. And by the way, speaking of dignity—

I write what I write, I said.

Was this part of the plan?

What plan?

The kidnapping.

I'm not sure I'm following you, Bob.

The abduction scenario, as you like to call it. Was this just a
ploy?

You mean did I abduct you in order to get a closer look? To spur
on my feeble imagination? Like those movie actors, the ones who
work at the assembly line at the General Motors plant for a day to
get inside the head of the working-class protagonist? Is that what
you mean, Bob? If so, no.

No?

And in any case, I said, there wasn't any full-scale plan. I don't do
full-scale plans. As you can probably tell by now, I'm not real good
at plot.

— —

Sure is a word that rarely comes out of my mouth; and whenever it
does, it usually connotes the opposite of what I'm feeling. In everyday speech, the word often comes right before the rhetorical question, *Why not?* As in a person who shrugs his shoulders and says,

Sure, why not? Let's meet your mother. And her mother, too. And maybe someone says that—just not me. Never. Or only when I feel myself trapped or otherwise coaxed into punishing myself and climbing back up on the cross. *Sure.*

That night—after hanging up the phone, ending the conversation with Promise about Robert Partnow, *the one who got kidnapped,* and her mother's impending visit—I'd gone immediately to the bedroom closet and taken the gun down from the shelf. I hadn't touched it since that April afternoon when I'd used it like a magic wand, to get what I wanted. Now it lay in my two hands, inert—and it stayed there, its cold turning warm. I closed my eyes, sniffed the barrel, and couldn't help but think of hard steel, its impenetrability. I imagined it as magical again, only this time more like a genie escaped from the bottle. Not asking so much as telling me what I wanted to do and when I wanted to do it.

— —

Bob and I were in the middle of watching *Prime Time Thursday.* We were letting the commercial featuring a red Dodge minivan play with the volume muted.

What if I said, professionally speaking, that you probably *should* be published?

What if you did?

And that life isn't fair, Bob said. And it definitely hasn't been fair in your case.

You're saying this, I asked, or it's as *if* you're saying this?

I'm saying it.

And so?

And so you're right in thinking you've gotten a raw deal.

Leaning back on his bunk bed with his hands clasped on top of his head, Bob had taken on a philosophical demeanor. And I decided to let him spin his thoughts about me and my failed life, even if I had no idea how this linked up with what we'd just been talking about—Mike Nichols and Diane Sawyer, Garry Trudeau and Jane Pauley. (Smart, talented men and their lapses of taste. How could it happen?)

You're a very good writer, Bob said—looking again at the television. We were still waiting to get back to Diane Sawyer's interview with Janet Jackson. *She may be the baby girl of the Jackson clan, but she is still her own woman—now more so than ever.*

I'm glad to hear it, I said.

And it's truly a shame you haven't been published. I mean, published in book form. It's not right and it's difficult to understand, given the last few frontlists I've seen.

I'm glad to hear it, Bob, but I didn't need to abduct you to figure that out.

Let's face it, he said—sighing. You don't know why the hell you kidnapped me.

— —

Voluntarily? I asked—perplexed by the question.

As an experiment, she said. You know, just to see what it would be like. How it would make you feel, or how it would make *her* feel.

Promise seemed to be asking the question in all sincerity, and so I stared at the librarian—a redhead roughly my own age, easily twenty pounds overweight, dressed in a blue denim jumper and a white turtleneck spotted with little red hearts—and I tried to imagine it. It was much easier than I might've anticipated: home from the library, a late-afternoon romp in her bedroom, a Raggedy Ann heirloom tossed from the bed to the floor, the hem of the jumper lifted up from behind, the cat meowing at the closed door.

No, I said. No. Not even as an experiment. Would Kafka?

Franz? You know the answer to that. But sometimes *I* do.

Do what?

Imagine sleeping with just about anyone.

Like kissing, I said.

No. Not like kissing. Not to be promiscuous. It has nothing to do with that. It's just that it might make someone happy. Making someone happy might be a kick.

Even if they knew you were doing it just to make them happy?

Well, no, obviously that wouldn't work, Promise said. That's why it only really works as a fantasy. But that's OK. In real life, you probably wouldn't want to kidnap a man and keep him in your basement.

As we sat there, and I thought about real life and its strange parameters, the librarian came out from behind the desk carrying a stack of magazines toward the periodicals area. With her glasses reflecting the fluorescent lights overhead, she looked like a schoolgirl with the magazines askance in her arms — she could've been holding a newborn, our child together, the consequence of a mercy fuck, and now it was too late. I was roped in.

And this seemed to sum up the difference between Promise and me — her fantasies ended happily, or at least with a happiness based on another's, whereas my fantasies always zoomed off in disastrous directions. It had been one of the few poignant discoveries of my life — that the word *fantasy* didn't always describe something you wanted to happen.

Do you even have a basement?

A basement? You mean, in my house?

Yes, Evan, in your house.

Of course, I said. Every house has a basement, doesn't it?

— —

Let's face it, he said — sighing. You don't know why the hell you kidnapped me. It's a mystery to you as well as to me, and it'll probably stay that way. But OK, let's take a wild guess here and say the abduction scenario has something to do with revenge.

What's your point?

It's a reasonable form of revenge, Bob said. Or that's not right, it's not *reasonable*. Wrong word.

It's *understandable,* I said.

Yes. Right. Given the circumstances, and from what I've seen of your writing, it's easy to understand your frustration.

And so if you'd read my novel-in-progress and it stunk, then my frustration would be *less* understandable?

Well, your novel doesn't stink.

Maybe it does, I said, and maybe it doesn't.

You think I'm lying?

Maybe. Or maybe you're speaking from the heart. But why should it matter anyway? What if the novel *is* good? So what? Does that absolve me of my crime?

— —

My favorite?

I needed to know what Promise meant by favorite. Did she mean my favorite woman to be with, to talk with? To spend a day with? Or simply my favorite, so far, to sleep with?

Take your pick, she whispered across the library table. And then, as though suddenly impatient, she proceeded to tell me about hers. Her favorite lover—the one, right after college, who somehow managed to take her *places she'd never gone before.* (At that point we could easily have put our heads together across the table and compared notes on the pleasures of surrender. I had a few stories of my own.) *Places never gone before,* she repeated—scrunching her lips up toward her nose, displeased with herself, embarrassed by her predictability. In Promise's opinion, women too often turned to men to take them places they'd never gone before, in bed or elsewhere. *Travel agents of the heart* is how she described these seductive apparitions.

Thirty minutes later—walking to my car after a long kiss in front of Promise's Toyota—I thought back on this conversation and realized I had no idea where Promise might want to go if, perchance, she acquiesced and let a man handle the travel arrangements. Where would I take her? Where might we go? The responsibility was weighing on me.

The question came back to me later—in the kitchen, before I'd gone down the stairs to see what Bob was doing. (Was he still there? Had he managed a nifty escape?) Flipping absentmindedly through the day's mail—including a forwarded letter of rejection for a story I forgot I'd ever submitted—I thought again about Promise and the specter of travel, and the risk of getting lost. And I realized that I'd always wanted to be the traveler and not the guide. I wanted to go someplace new, to be taken there, led by the hand, even blindfolded if it came to that. I imagined it literally, then—Promise blindfolding me and putting me in her little Toyota and driving for hours to a secret destination; and finally when she removed the piece of silk, lifted it from my eyes, I would find myself someplace sublime— which meant just about anywhere other than where I'd ever been before.

This flight of fancy was, then, my own escape.

— —

When do I get to see the rest?

There's only two more chapters, I said. So far.

Hand them over, Bob said—barking the words, playing the aggressor, making my acquiescence a formality.

— —

What if I want to kiss you? I said.

Sounds good to me.

Right now. Right now I want to kiss you.

Well, buckaroo, that's pretty much impossible, isn't it?

I guess it is, I said—making myself sound very sad, even though I was.

Promise and I were talking on the telephone again, a few hours after parting outside the library. There, sitting at the table, we'd mostly confined our words to the page. Now, talking on the phone, I realized how much I depended on her face—its expression, the intricacies of her smile, the lift of her eyebrows—in order to find my bearings, to make the silences something other than occasions for paranoia.

Do you own a gun?

You're very good at the question out of the blue, I said. Has anyone ever told you that?

Has anyone told you you're good at sidestepping questions?

OK, I said. In fact I do own a gun.

Good.

Good?

For what purpose, Evan? Self-protection?

I'd just always wanted to own a gun. So I went out and bought one.

Where? Where did you buy it?

New Jersey.

Why do these things always happen in New Jersey?

It's not loaded, I said. The gun, I don't keep it loaded.

That makes sense.

It does?

It's like a camera without film, she said. When I was a girl I really wanted a camera and my father gave me an old one of his. A Minolta SLR, I remember. It didn't work but I loved it anyway, and I went around taking pictures all day long. I can still hear the sound of the mirror, like a clucking tongue.

I waited, and sure enough—Promise made the sound over the phone. And right then I saw what I'd still not seen but only touched—the wet bottom of her tongue, its tight little frenum, and the whole soft wonder of *mucous membrane*.

No film, I said. What was the point?

I was just five years old, maybe six. At the time I didn't care. I was taking imaginary pictures. Are you shooting imaginary people, Evan?

All the time, I said—clearing my throat.

— —

I just worry, I said.

About what?

I don't know. Motives?

Let me ask you something, Bob said—getting closer now, leaning a shoulder into the chain-link fence, which bowed with his
weight. I was a little scared in that moment, our bodies just a step
away from each other. I also felt proud, though—the bottom of the
fence, buried in cement, held firm.

Ask away, I said—still thinking about Promise, her motives,
about how intimacy seemed like a minefield of combustible needs
and desires.

When you first met Promise at the library—

I mentioned her name?

You did a minute ago, Bob said.

I'm beginning to forget what I've said, what I haven't.

When you first met her, he said, did it ever cross your mind to
take advantage of her? You know, force the issue.

Force what issue? I asked—standing there with hands in my
trouser pockets, the toes of my shoes touching the base of the
fence.

I'm just asking. Asking whether you ever thought of taking her
by force, whether—

What, as a romantic ploy?

OK, my mistake, Bob said—pulling back from the fence and
holding his hands up, crisscrossed at the wrists. My mistake. I
just—

Rape? I said.

Not exactly rape—

You think I'm capable of—

Excuse me, Evan, you know, but you *do* tend to force things.
There's a small matter of precedent here.

I didn't rape you, I said.

I wasn't claiming that you did. I was just worried about the girl.

I *like* this girl, I said.

OK. So go for it. How old is she?

Twenty-five.

She's an adult, Bob said. Invite her over for a drink.

Invite her *here*?

Why not?

— —

Last night, Promise said — over the phone. You know what I did last night?

No.

I tried to imagine what it would be like to be you.

Why?

I was working on the novel.

The one you won't show me, I said. The one with me and the older woman.

Yes.

What's her name?

None of your business, Promise said. And I decided I needed to concentrate more. On *you*. I mean, not in terms of reality, of what you're like right now. But in terms of imagination. Imagining you. Imagining *being* you.

Not being able to imagine being me. That was one of the downsides, I thought, of having already taken on the unlucky assignment.

And so what was it like? I asked. To be me. What did I do or think or say?

You know I'm superstitious that way, she said. But I *can* tell you that I wrote for two solid hours and you really came to life.

Do I have a name yet?

No. But you have red hair, I can tell you that.

Why?

Why? You're a writer, Evan. You should know why.

Let me guess.

Because it *is* red, Promise said — beating me to the punch.

I could only smile, reach a hand up and run it through my hair and imagine that, yes, it *was* red. And my skin was stenciled now with freckles, too.

God, is that insulting? she said. I mean, to just give you red hair, arbitrarily. Because that's what I'm doing. I see you with red hair, Evan.

What else?

Secrets, she said. You've got quite a lot of those.

— • —

You're just saying that.

I'm not, Bob said. I mean it. Listen, if you ever get past this whole kidnapping thing—

It's only a draft, I said. It's not finished.

I know that, Evan. I read drafts all the time, remember? I'm pretty good at seeing beyond the draft, looking toward the finished book. Or at least I was pretty good at it thirty-one days ago.

And my book, I said, what makes it good?

I'm particularly impressed with how you're able to create a well-defined relationship between the editor and the failed writer.

Thanks.

The descriptions of the basement are first-rate.

All of it passes for reality?

Yes, Bob said. Definitely. It's a minor detail, but I'm not sure it's necessary to make the television any bigger than it already is. And why not give the narrator a real name?

For a moment Bob and I simply stared at each other through the chain-link fence—the silence elongating. And I wanted to say *thank you*. I wanted to say that I *did* believe him and that it meant a lot to me. But that would've sounded a little facile, no?

One criticism, Bob finally said—holding up a single finger. I mean, besides the fact that you've painted Lloyd too broadly, relied too much on stereotype. And you're not going to like me saying this. But I think the novel is missing an ingredient. It needs a love interest.

For Bob?

For the narrator.

I've thought about that, I said.

And one more thing, and this I shouldn't say, Bob said—interrupting himself, clearing his throat.

— ·—

You know what my mother would say?

We were standing in the foyer of my house—a small space just inside the door that served as a location for a heating vent in the floor. A pair of my shoes sat to the left of that vent. With her mother's impending visit, Promise had been talking about her a lot.

Excuse me for saying this, Promise said—her voice higher, more like a child's than a mother's—*but where's the furniture?*

Right then and there I looked around my living room and realized that yes, especially from a mother's point of view, I might've gone too far with the minimalist aesthetic—driven more by frugality, really, than taste. There was a chair, a small table, and a lot of empty space, particularly in front of the fireplace. For practical reasons, I'd invested my decorating dollars in the basement. Upstairs, I was living mostly with the bedroom furniture of my childhood—stuff I'd dragged around since college.

She's right, your mother, I said. She's totally right.

Promise frowned and shook her head. We were in cahoots, she seemed to be saying—partners in the hidden subtleties of interior decorating; and her mother was on the outside looking in—some old, sad dog rubbing its wet nose on the window.

The bottom line, it suddenly occurred to me—irrespective of mothers, their aesthetics—was that we couldn't really sit down in the living room. And so, led by circumstance into the kitchen, Promise and I took seats at the Formica table I'd picked up at a yard sale the first weekend after my move to Sandhurst. And yes, it did feel odd to have another person there; many a day I'd sat and imagined an unshackled Bob across the way, spooning cornflakes and reading the morning paper.

I have a secret to tell you, Promise said—playing idly with the salt and pepper shakers. Made of Waterford crystal, handed down by my grandmother and then my mother, they were completely out of keeping with the rest of the kitchen.

A secret?

My mother's coming for a visit.

You already—

And there's absolutely *no* reason that you should have to meet her, she said—shaking her head. I don't want to force you to do that. You have better things to do, I'm sure.

Like what?

But here's the thing, Promise said. I sort of want to see the two of you in the same room. I need you there, together. To watch you.

Watch me what?

Not *you*. The two of you. Together. Because I'm writing about you and my mother. Together.

Together?

It's just fiction, she said—shaking her head. That doesn't make you uncomfortable, does it? Because if it makes you uncomfortable—

What do I do when I meet your mother?

Whatever you want, she said—eyebrows dipping. I shouldn't have even brought this up. It's just that I felt like I should. Should—

Should disclose it, I said. Writer to writer.

Or maybe I *wanted* to, she said—setting the salt and pepper shakers back to their original positions, flush with the wall. I know we just sat down, Evan, but now I'm curious. About the rest. The rest of the house. Do I get a tour?

And so we were up again, on our feet.

— —

And one more thing, and this I shouldn't say, Bob said—interrupting himself, clearing his throat.

Staring at this man on the other side of the chain-link fence, I waited while he paused; and what did I expect to hear? What was it he was going to say even if he shouldn't? I hoped it was going to be about *us,* about Bob and me, about some good that had come from his confinement. Didn't *that* need to be a part of the story, too?

The kidnapping, Bob said, and the eventual publicity of my release and then the release of your name as the kidnapper, these things are *not* going to hurt your chances.

Chances?

With a lesser book, he said—and he looked down at the manuscript, pages now askew in his lap—it might be difficult. But this is a sensational beginning. Really, it is. And with the inevitable media attention, I think your chances of getting somewhere, of achieving a bit of literary notoriety, are good. Even very good. It's certainly a start.

And so what are you—

It's a marketing director's dream, he said.

But what are you saying, Bob?

It may be a sad commentary on our culture—

Are you saying that *you'll* publish it?

Bob looked at me now and smiled. And again I found myself waiting, trying not to give away the pain of hanging on his every word. At first I had no idea what he was going to say. Then, suddenly, I did have an idea. And almost smiling, I readied myself to tell Bob yet again that I wasn't as stupid and gullible as he might think.

Evan, he said, imagine the precedent of an editor publishing an author who kidnaps him. I don't think so. And especially when the editor is more than a little pissed.

Pissed?

Just to remind you, he said. I appreciate—

You're still pissed?

Let's just say I appreciate your goodwill. But this hasn't exactly been my idea of a vacation.

I glanced at the manuscript, as Bob dropped it between his feet. And I felt like the child of dashed hopes. I couldn't help thinking

of vacations, the only kind I'd experienced as a kid—sitting in the
backseat of the Buick, waving at cigarette smoke with one hand and
holding a deck of cards in the other. My lone source of amusement:
card tricks where I was both the con and the mark.

And so that wasn't my point, Bob said.

I didn't think it was, I said—clearing my throat. I was just asking.

— —

And so we were up again, on our feet. Promise seemed more relaxed
upstairs, looking at my collection of stuffed monkeys—twenty-one
in all. She smiled and said she hadn't realized I was so sentimental. She stared long and hard at a picture of my mother and father
hung in the hallway, just to the left of his diploma from Western
Wisconsin Agricultural College. I expected her to say that I looked
like neither, but she said nothing; I expected her to express surprise
that I'd display my father's diploma, but she didn't. In the bedroom
she ran her hand over the rough texture of the tapestry woven in
rich shades of red, hanging on the wall above my bed. It was a gift,
I explained. Promise nodded, looked down and pushed on my bed
with her hand, twice, like a customer at Mancini's Sleepworld. Or
was she like a woman who might rush pell-mell toward intercourse?

Having traveled downstairs again, we stood in the kitchen.
Leaning against a wall, Promise smiled at me—and there was something about the leaning that put me at ease. I smiled back, used both
hands to brace myself against the refrigerator.

The basement? she said.

I reached with one hand and pointed to the door in the corner of
the kitchen, directly behind her, on the other side of the stove. Then
I turned my attention to what passed, in my modest abode, for the
liquor cabinet—to the left of the refrigerator.

Was it this particular basement, Promise asked, that inspired you?

That's sort of an autobiographical question, isn't it?

I guess it is. May I? she asked—motioning toward the door when
I looked over at her; and I nodded my head.

But, of course, the door was locked. And when Promise came to that conclusion, after a few turns of the handle, she looked back at me with a show of narrowed eyes—a pantomime of frustration.

Would you like a drink? I asked—lifting a bottle of Seagram's.

I'd be honored, Mr. Ulmer. So then, no basement?

No, it's there. It's just locked up. It's a very untidy situation down there. You know how basements are.

Like closets, Promise said. Like laundry hampers. Like kitchen sinks full of plates after a cooking binge.

Yes.

Embarrassing?

Yes, I said.

Messy?

Right.

And you're referring to the abductee and his conditions of squalor? she asked—smiling.

I finished the pouring and added ice, and I shook the concoction in one hand. Not for the first time, the motion was disquieting—a little too near, too dear, this jerky movement—and so I hurried the process. With false aplomb, I presented Promise with a dry martini. It was a drink I'd come to enjoy, in spite of all my efforts to reject my father's favorite means of withdrawal.

Where's yours?

I make them one at a time, I said—giving away too much about what it's like to be a man who lives alone.

Promise sat down at the table and took a sip of her martini, and then another. What do you think it means, she asked, that we're drinking together?

Versus what? Eating together?

Versus holding in our hands the reins, she said. Keeping in control. *When butterflies renounce their drams, I shall but drink the more!* That's Dickinson getting drunk on life.

Still making my own martini, I turned my head and looked over. She must've thought I wouldn't understand the reference because she had her hands in front of her as though she were rid-ing a stagecoach, yanking back on the reins. The horses, obedient to the wrenching, stopped in their tracks and kicked up a good deal of dust. I shook and shook and poured the liquid into the second glass. Icy strands formed a thin layer on the surface—perfect.

Here's to spirited horses, I said—raising my glass.

Did you say *houses* or *horses*?

Horses.

You're beginning to spook me, Evan Ulmer, she said—taking another sip. And I really do want to go down to that basement. Could we arrange such a trip?

A trip? For what purpose?

To see.

To see what?

To see what makes Evan Ulmer tick. What stirs his imagination. Basements are a kind of metaphor, don't you think? Or they can be.

Dark places, I said—sipping.

8

◀◯▶

Who was Evan Ulmer? *That was Promise's question. And it seemed like one that more people might've asked. Strange, wasn't it, that no one entertained this question nearly as much as I did? How do you square your own interest in yourself with others' relative indifference? That was what I remember feeling as a child—overwhelmed by life, asking questions that seemed inappropriate and foreign to those around me. No surprise, but I was* a nervous *child, overcome with the project of daily life—making sure my shoes were tied, my zipper in the upright position, my thoughts safely within the borders of my porous little mind.*

Growing up in Appleton, an only child, it would've helped to have someone else, another worrier or a person with whom to pore over my list of questions and experience the pleasure of not *answering them. My mother? She didn't particularly like questions—asking them, answering them, evading them. My father had a habit, which only got worse with age, of feigning curiosity, asking questions for the purpose of answering them himself. Did he really care whether I liked bebop jazz? No, not really, but he had some strong opinions about it himself. It always seemed crazy to me, beside the point—like asking a girl back to your hotel room and then whacking off in the bathroom.*

*I*T'S TIME, ISN'T IT? These words kept running through my mind. I might as well have had them tattooed on my forehead — to remind myself, while shaving, of the thing I couldn't forget. Just in case. *It's time.* Time to what? And when exactly, and why?

For perhaps the first time in my life, I was writing daily and with some confidence. Words were rushing this way and that—a procession, a scattered cavalcade—and I was grabbing whichever ones I wanted. My novel was getting closer to being finished. Was this productivity a matter of Bob's opinion, his generous speculations on the context of my book's publication? Was it a matter of sitting across a library table from someone equally crazy and doubly ambitious every day? Did it have to do with that same person kissing me, *wanting* to kiss me? Was each kiss, an inspiration, bearing the fruit of a subsequent chapter?

In any case, I felt that something had grown, expanded, and now it needed to be released. *It's time, isn't it?* It's silly to say, silly even to think—but I imagined myself as pregnant, as having given myself over to a process, provided it the means to make its own way in the world. Sometimes it was me—I was the one to be released, as though I had graduated from some long, grueling purgatory. (*Liberated* is the wrong word. An act of beneficence this wasn't.) But more often it was Bob. He'd already been making his way in the world; and yet I imagined—without too much hubris, I hoped—a future in which he'd make the most of the abduction scenario.

There *was* a countercurrent in my mind, a flip side of my eagerness to give Bob his walking papers. I was hard at work, after all, and I wanted to finish my novel before too much dust got unsettled. And I was getting close—tantalizingly so. When I told Promise, she seemed happy for me, but she also said she wanted to see the manuscript. And she still wanted to have a look at the basement that had supposedly inspired my work.

— —

Promise's mother arrived on Tuesday and left on Thursday. I met her on Wednesday evening, after dinner.

In the living room, as I sat across from them in the rocker with the maimed teddy bear in my lap, my mind was a caldron; it had been bubbling since I walked through the front door and shook hands with Margaret, almost tripping over Hans who was zooming back and forth between us, his wet black nose a conduit. My mind was doing its own zooming—my thoughts were running circles around whatever reality the conversation might've had. It was disconcerting to see Margaret, Promise's mother, with her small nipples pressing against her blue, skin-tight Lycra top. Wasn't that the kind of shirt that bicyclists wore? In any case, wasn't this attire reserved for much younger women?

Physically speaking, Margaret was a lot like her daughter—older, of course. Prettier, too. Same hair, same proud nose, same forehead given to expressions of perplexity; and the same chin, the sharpness of which, until I saw it twice, I hadn't really noticed before. But I could never have anticipated her voice. (I told you so, Promise said later—but I must have forgotten her mention of it.) It was like a child's, her voice, or more a parody of a child's—an adult's version of what a child's might sound like. I found myself talking to Margaret with a limited vocabulary, as though speaking to a ten-year-old. Until I realized she was often a step ahead of me.

My voice—that's the one I've never got used to. Not that I was doing a lot of talking. In fact, Margaret asked me few questions. She didn't seem particularly hungry for information. She was hardly a protective mother grilling the new man in her daughter's life. (I'm embarrassed to put it that way—I don't know that I've been a man in *anyone's* life, not even my own.) Margaret seemed too oblivious to be suspicious, too undaunted, too used to getting what she wanted. She resembled her daughter, but she possessed little of the strange and wonderful curiosity that had drawn me to Promise.

— —

So what was K.'s problem exactly?

Bob was reading *The Castle*. The week before I'd bought a second copy and given it to him. He said he'd read it once, long ago at Princeton, but couldn't really remember it.

I frowned as I asked my question, about the nature of K.'s problem, as though trying to draw on my own higher education. I didn't mention that only a couple of days ago I'd finished reading Kafka's novel. I'm not sure why I lied about this, such a small thing. Keeping deceit alive in the midst of its death throes?

You want the official answer, Bob said, or do you want *my* answer?

Yours.

He can't get the girls, can't get into that damn castle, and like a good Jew he takes it lying down.

That's a little harsh, isn't it? I asked—even though I couldn't have summed it up any better myself.

You asked.

Of course, I said.

Maybe I have this wrong, but there's a passage that goes something like, *We have a saying here and maybe you've heard it. Official decisions are as shy as girls.*

As shy as *young* girls, I said. Yes, I remember. Signifying?

The guy's going in circles, Bob said. His mind's a mess. He can't get anywhere.

So what if we imagined K. with an attitude? I asked. You know, a little spunk.

Spunk?

K. with a boner, I said. A *big* boner. Would that get him to the castle?

I hadn't thought of—

I'm speaking metaphorically, Bob. He's doomed. He's a loser. He can't muster the strength.

It's not a pretty picture, Bob said, that's true enough. To be honest, the book's depressing me. I'm finding it a hard read. Maybe it's sitting in this cage and—

You really don't like to read, do you?

— —

For Neil and me, and I know Promise feels this way, too, Margaret said, Sandhurst has always been a special place. It's changed. *We've* changed. We're older now, Evan. But it really doesn't matter. Because when I walk into *this* house, I feel relaxed. Immediately. It's like a drug, a warm feeling all over my body.

Promise, sitting next to her mother on the couch, shot me a look—which I had enough presence of mind to ignore.

And what about you, Evan? What brought you to this lovely spot? Was it simply the contrast between the peacefulness, here, and New York with all of its noise and dust?

I like noise and dust, I said, but—

Did you come here to write like Promise?

Yes. That's why I did come.

And so what was like for you, coming?

Good, I said. It's a nice place to—

Were you running away, too?

Running away? I said.

Promise was running away. Weren't you, darling? You don't mind me saying that, do you? It's only my opinion.

You can say anything you want, Promise said.

This is *my* interpretation, Margaret said—looking at me, then smiling. Her eyes, unlike her daughter's, kept their shape when she smiled. I was waiting to hear the interpretation, but then again maybe I'd already heard it. Or maybe she wanted me to ask more questions.

I think Promise needed to get away from her parents, she finally said—picking up the thread. I know that's how I felt when I was Promise's age. She's deciding who she wants to become. And she's becoming quite an interesting young woman, wouldn't you agree?

Yes, I said.

Then you see what I mean, Margaret said—nodding slowly, yanking down one of the Lycra sleeves that had crept into her armpit.

— —

You really don't like to read, do you?

Bob opened his mouth to respond, and then he worked his lips into the silly grin of a man who was exposed but unapologetic— a expression I could never produce.

It's part of the job, he finally said.

I read about it, I said. In *Publishers Weekly*.

Read what?

About editors who—

Lose their taste for reading? Bob said. Yes, I read that article, too. It happens. Or it *can* happen. I remember that article, and it was like reading about memory loss or adult ADD. You end up wondering whether it's an article about you. And maybe it *was* about me. I didn't really think about it that much at the time. But now, having suffered this particular indignity—

It's given you a new perspective?

Being held here like an animal, Bob said, it's made me think twice.

Like an *animal*?

Against my will. It's made me realize what counts, and how maybe it's time to move on.

Move on?

Yes, he said. End it. You know, my career as estimable editor. Do something else. Get out from under all those words. I mean, *maybe*.

I don't know. I don't like to think I've ended your career.

No reason to flatter yourself, Bob said.

— —

Our wineglasses were empty now.

What about you? I said.

I felt odd asking—not because it was an especially prying question. But for the first half-hour of this nonstop conversation between her mother and me, Promise had been monitoring the two of us like we were a lab experiment, a couple of mice in turmoil. *Older* mice, I couldn't help thinking. I was closer to Margaret's age than to Promise's. It made me a little nervous.

Me? Margaret said—turning her head away, shyly, so I could see only half of her face. I'm a strange one, I'm afraid.

Out of the corner of my eye I spied Promise rolling her eyes. *No joke,* she was saying without words.

I don't believe in God, Margaret said, but I go to church every Sunday. I attend the Riverside Church. Do you know it? It's the most *beautiful* church in all of America.

This from an intelligent woman, Promise said, who hasn't visited more than four of our fifty states in her life.

Of course some of the cathedrals of Europe are stunning, she said. Anyway, Owen, it's a very interesting question you ask about religion.

It's Evan, mother.

I *said* Evan.

You said Owen.

Are you an atheist? I asked—trying to move things along, to neutralize Promise, even though the question struck me as impolite.

Technically, yes, Margaret said. But I just love the hymns, the atmosphere, the wooden pews, the chance to wear hats in a world that mostly frowns on them. And sometimes, every now and then, I wish I *did* believe.

Who's frowning? Promise said—furrowing her brow to demonstrate, or maybe out of exasperation.

Looking back and forth between the two of them—these Buckley women with their strong jaws, their full lips, their pert nipples—I found Promise's digs at her mother tiring. For once, Promise's age was showing—the effect, I guessed, of a relatively recent separation. Perhaps Margaret was right in saying her daughter had run away, was in the process of becoming.

On the couch, the two women now stared at each other, their expressions blank—at least as far as I could tell—and disconcerting because of it. My gaze shifted back and forth, and I imagined them having a secret, silent conversation, as though they were genetically connected beings in a science-fiction movie where words had become superfluous artifacts. I was trying to gauge this moment, this bit of silence, when Hans lifted his head and glanced at me. Was he also confused? I looked back at him, tempted to shrug my shoulders in solidarity.

Promise tells me you're writing a book.

Yes, I said.

What's it about?

It's about failure, I said—trying for spontaneity.

Is it autobiographical?

— —

Friday night, after *Nightline* and a concomitant conversation with Bob about the perils of Ecstasy, I went upstairs and sat on my bed. I flipped through a few magazines. Restless, I imagined Promise and me, each in our own bedrooms. It was like a split-screen experiment in a movie, an exercise in narrative omniscience. And what was Promise doing? Was she writing? Taking pleasure in the wonder of words, feeling their power? (Was there pleasure in doing what you had to do?) Or was she indulging in baser forms of bodily ecstasy?

Down in his own makeshift bedroom, Bob was probably up to the same thing—wanking, not writing. Bob had dismissed my suggestion that he pen a short memoir, and he always talked about his one-time authorial aspirations the way I might speak of once having wanted to be President of the United States. Editors, he'd told me in a candid moment, make awful writers—a notch below journalists.

(He mentioned Michael Korda and—it was true—we both winced.) Bob's contempt for his own kind was becoming clearer, and he seemed to have let down his professional defenses. And I was obviously feeling more trusting—otherwise I wouldn't have shown him the additional chapters of my manuscript.

But when would I show my work to Promise? And more interestingly, considering the subject matter of her work, when would she show me hers? Why hadn't it happened already? It was cruel, given the proximity of her words—I'd look across the library table, day after day, at the pages of her journal covered with secret scribbles. Each word a choice, an act of ardor. I imagined those pages as love letters written to someone else. Or maybe they were addressed to absolutely no one. But what I couldn't imagine—sitting on my bed that night, restless—was that they were written to me. *About* me, yes. But *to* me?

— —

Do you see what I'm saying? Promise said to me over the telephone, the day after her mother left. I'm speaking hypothetically.

I was noticing how, at moments like this, Promise could sound very formal. She was pleading with her words, not with her tone. Never any coldness in her voice—just this methodical way of putting words together that emphasized the spaces between them. I imagined it as her father's voice as he paced back and forth in the courtroom, imploring the jury, making his case. It certainly wasn't her mother's voice.

Think about all the times in your life, Promise said, when you've just really, really wanted something. You wouldn't let yourself get it, and then later you saw how stupid it was. I mean, that you stopped yourself. Do you see what I'm saying?

She was in her upstairs bedroom—I could tell from the strange, soft acoustics produced by the wall-to-wall carpeting. In my own upstairs bedroom, I lay on my unmade bed and stared across the room at the same pine bureau in which I'd stored my clothes as a fifteen-year-old. A transistor radio, a relic from that same period, lay next to a nearly empty Perrier bottle.

Our ears pressed against black cordless phones, Promise and I occupied a place that was barely conterminous to the real world. At any rate, that was my impression of what we had in common—the tendency to find alternate worlds within *this* world. Was I wrong about that? We were like a pair of children who, bent toward curiosity, might remove the screws, let them drop and scatter, and take a good long look at the inside of that transistor radio.

In short, Promise was saying that now she wanted to fuck.

—▪—

OK, so let's get this one thing straight, I said—from my side of the fence. I am *not* asking you to talk about your daughters.

Of course you are.

I'm just asking why you don't want to.

That's easy enough to imagine, Bob said.

Imagine? Imagine what?

Don't be dense, Evan. I'm in the news. My wife is in the news, Lloyd is in the news. That can't be easy for either of them—

Lloyd seems to be basking in it.

When I get back, there's going to be a certain amount of work to be done.

Repair work, I said.

Yes. Right.

Is it that you think your daughters are angry?

This is exactly what I don't want to talk about, Bob said—turning his face away, toward the wall, like a stubborn child.

I'm sorry, sorry for all this, I said—and when he turned and looked at me, I spun my finger in a circle, like a little fly buzzing above my head. Everything, all of it. Keeping you here, taking you away, making your daughters angry.

I didn't say they were angry, Bob said. You're not the right person, that's what I'm saying. I'll talk to you about this and that. I'll read your manuscript. I'll tell you about the publishing world. I'll tell you about Claudia and Lloyd. I don't even always know why. Because maybe I'm lonely or because what the hell difference does it make. But I'm not going to talk to you about my daughters. I've made that decision.

I respect that, I said—and I meant it. I imagine you're a wonderful father.

I *am* a wonderful father.

Everyone's complex, I said. Everyone's got secrets. One of my mother's sisters committed suicide, but no one ever told any of us. My father had a secret stash of pornography, and some of it involved farm animals.

And was he wonderful? Your father?

No. But—

I'm not your father, Evan.

Jesus, I wasn't—

And I've got another headache, Bob said.

Are you out of pills?

I didn't expect to be kidnapped and hear Peter Jennings speculating about my sexuality on the nightly news, that's what I'm saying. I hadn't foreseen that that might happen.

Yes, and then along came Evan Ulmer, I said—hanging my head, giving it a feeble shake, thinking that it should be *me*. If anyone deserved a headache, it was me.

It's not fun to watch your life being scrutinized, Bob said. You'll see. When this is over, one way or the other, Evan Ulmer will become a household name, at least in New York City. The *Times* will have quotes from clinical psychologists on what exactly went wrong with Evan Ulmer. Maybe they'll say it was the farm animals. Diane Sawyer will sit on Promise's sofa and ask her personal questions about Evan Ulmer and about why—

Let's not talk about Promise, OK? Is that fair?

—◄—►—

In bed, awake but barely—an increasingly common zone these days—I didn't feel like getting up to look for a magazine I hadn't already read. And it was a little too early to go downstairs to see if Bob, too, was awake. Probably he wasn't, considering how long and deeply he'd been sleeping the past few days. No matter what the time, I might hear that phlegmy snore of his before I got halfway down the stairs.

My mind wandered over the territory of girls I'd known as a boy. The ones I couldn't get to, the most popular girls in Appleton. You lost out and you never knew exactly why. It was a preamble to adult life—my first rejection slips, as it were. And why did the memory of these girls always come back to me? Why were their names forever etched on the tender lining of my brain? Robin, Cindy, Becky, Teri—terribly illicit, wholesome Wisconsin girls. Girls I'd barely known, girls I'd never touched or talked to at any length.

Maybe it never happened because you wanted it to happen. Especially back then, wanting seemed dangerous—like a prophecy fulfilling itself, perversely, in reverse. I tried to keep my wants to a minimum; and when I was a believer, I prayed for things sparingly.

Very early morning, first light creeping through the shades, Bob down below, in thrall to his dreams—at that moment, the past was hanging over me like an ominous cloud. It warned me of the mistakes I'd already made. Is it just me who feels sometimes that it might be possible to go back, to think things through and change things that have, in retrospect, taken on an air of inevitability?

But then time snaps back, and the old logic takes over—*maybe it never happened because you wanted it to happen.* Regret has always worked that way—a door to the past, but invariably there's a price of admission. Sleeplessness, usually.

— —

In short, Promise was saying that now she wanted to fuck.

In the midst of a conversation about intimacy—about how it had a mind of its own, how it transgressed normal borders and made a mockery of safety—she'd spoken of this contiguity as a *hypothetical convergence*. Fucking was a metaphor. Or was it?

But I thought—

What? What, Evan?

I thought you wanted to go slow, I said.

Slow, she said. Fast. The one follows the other, doesn't it? It's like an impulse, isn't it? It's like jumping into a pool of very cold water. You think I'm crazy?

Crazy, no, I'm just surprised, I said.

I was on my stomach, looking over the edge of the bed, visualizing the water below. I was trying to imagine what an impulse—to jump, or *not* to jump—might feel like. Except for taking Bob into captivity, and kissing Promise that day in the park, I'd never acted impulsively. Even so, right then I was feeling the impulse to bring up Margaret and ask Promise whether her mother's visit had anything to do with this new emphasis on impulse. But I didn't.

Even after we returned to our original topic—suburbia as a killer of romance and passion—and after I reached over the side of the bed and returned the phone to its cradle on the floor, there was something there. Something palpable at the back of my throat where words are always their own masters. These words, these thoughts—it felt as if they were escaping in the wrong direction, going further and deeper, burrowing *in*. I cleared my throat, rose to my feet, swallowed some dead water from the Perrier bottle atop the bureau. I went down the hall to the bathroom and found a tissue and blew my nose. And I could feel my heart beating. I'd already jumped and felt the bone chill—always a shock, no matter how long you've seen it coming.

9

My mother told me one morning, when I was still a child, The worst about you is the best. *Or maybe it was the other way around. It's funny what you remember, what you don't. In any case, the moment stuck with me. My father, I remember, was reading the* Journal Sentinel, *one hand holding the paper, the other smearing toast with egg yolk. Prejudiced against forks and other niceties, he always plied his piece of burnt bread like a dry sponge.*

At the time I didn't know what my mother meant. And my father, intent on his breakfast, probably didn't much care. I really wanted to know. Now it's too late, or maybe my curiosity has waned. But back then, as a child, I liked the syntax of paradox. Everything was a puzzle to me, a conundrum—a dilemma. On first learning the meaning of dilemma, *I'd wondered whether the word had been expressly created to describe the state—caught somewhere in the middle—that I so often found myself in. It seemed that language, especially the newest words, had a way of finding me. Or finding me* out, *reading my mind.*

Maybe my mother had been speaking of her mixed blessing—the best son, the worst son. *The son you hadn't wanted, but learned to love. We had that in common, my mother and me—this tendency to see our messy lives as handed down, our affections composed from afar. That and holding onto habits and attitudes that were long past their usefulness.*

A T EIGHT-THIRTY in the evening, I opened the door to the stairs to the basement. Sitting down on the top step, I put my head on the pedestal of my hands and closed my eyes. I thought about what I was doing, or what I was *thinking* of doing. (Always that distinction—action like thought pushed off the edge of a cliff.) Was it time?

Down below Bob was on his treadmill. I knew as much because the television was particularly loud. I could hear intro music giving way to silence, and then the voice of Jane Pauley. *In an age when nothing, it seems, is too painful to talk about, what you're about to see remains an exception. It's a problem rarely discussed, even though millions struggle with it, usually beginning in adolescence. And because no one talks about it, many believe they are suffering alone. That's how one young woman felt when it happened to her. She lost her emotional footing and plunged into a black hole of anxiety and despair. Dateline followed her for nearly a year through a remarkable journey from the path of self-destruction to the promise of recovery. Here's Dawn Fratangelo.*

Had it been a remarkable journey? Was it time to call it quits? And if so, what was I quitting? I asked myself these questions, feeling as though I'd slipped my way into one of Bob's self-help books—struggling against demons, strategizing recovery. I felt alone, very alone, sitting there; Jane Pauley had put me in the wrong mood for anything other than anxiety and despair. Action seemed beyond me.

I stood up, went through the kitchen, and climbed the stairs to my bedroom. I took the gun down from the closet shelf. With the weapon cradled in my palm, I touched the small screws near the trigger guard. *One, two, three, four.* I found and inspected a series of small imperfections, tiny pits, in the surface of the cylinder. As though checking for dust, I ran a finger along the words *Colt Python* that were engraved on the barrel. An unnecessary fuddling of animal species, wasn't that?

— —

I bet you thought I was the UPS guy, Promise said—when I opened the front door.

It's a little late in the day for—

Well, I'm dressed for the role, she said—spinning around to show off her stiff cotton dress, a solid brown. In a perverse way, it made me think more of the SS than UPS. It wasn't every day that Promise appeared on my doorstep. I found it unnerving, especially since I was just on my way out.

It's very becoming, I said.

Anyway, I was in the neighborhood. Isn't that what they say? What *one* says? *I was just in the neighborhood.* Of course, it makes no sense in this case, since I pretty much live in your neighborhood.

And I live in yours.

Hi, neighbor, she said—hand held up in a wave. Are you going somewhere? Going out?

Going out?

You're wearing a jacket.

I am? I said—lowering my chin. I guess I am.

Aren't you going to ask me in?

Of course, I said. Yes, I'm sorry. Come in.

And I swung the front door wide open. It was only as she swept by me in her brown dress, cinched at the waist with a worn leather belt, that I remembered the weapon in the pocket of my cotton jacket.

As Promise told me about a trip to the vet's office with Hans earlier that day—strife in the waiting room, two cats clawing each other—she climbed the stairs and I followed. Where were we going?

Apparently into my bedroom. And soon enough we were lying side by side on my bed, staring at the ceiling and talking like kids at a sleepover. It took five minutes and one kiss before I spilled my guts. Her hand in mine, I spit out my big secret without so much as a prelude.

No, Promise said—her head turning back and forth on the pillow.

Yes.

No.

Yes, I said.

I just don't believe you.

Now I regret having said anything, I said—speaking the truth, wishing that I'd restrained myself, given us a chance to do more than kick off our shoes and lie down on my bed. After all, she was wearing a dress, and I hadn't explored the underneath. I still had my jacket on, my pocket bulging.

Metaphorically, she said—letting go of my hand and propping herself up on one elbow.

What?

You mean metaphorically he's down there. You mean—

I'm not much for metaphors, I said. I've never been able to figure out the difference between a metaphor, an analogy, and a simile. Maybe if I'd gone to Yale—

Prove it.

Prove what?

Show me, she said.

Yes, of course I will, I said—reaching over and touching the curve of her left ear, imagining that she was deaf and hadn't heard a word I'd said about the goings-on in the basement.

In a matter of seconds, Promise had knocked my hand away and jumped off the bed. She stood there, one hip thrust out, playfully wagging a finger at me, and then she pointed that finger at the rug under her feet. She was alluding, I knew, to the world two stories below.

Now? I said—clearing my throat, noticing that perhaps Promise wasn't so unused to getting what she wanted.

Now.

— —

Bob looked at one of us, then the other, his gaze moving back and forth as though we were in tennis whites whacking a ball across a taut net. I recognized the pattern—Bob reacting warily to both good and bad news, looking for signs that something wasn't as it seemed, even as he offered no resistance. Belatedly, as usual, I'd begun to plumb the depths of Bob's psychology.

Mr. Partnow?

Yes.

Hello, Mr. Partnow. I'm Promise Buckley.

It's Bob, I said. Call him Bob.

Bob, she said. Hello.

Bob looked at us with utter stillness, his eyes a picture of sufferance—like a dog standing elbow-deep in a bathtub.

Bob's pissed at me, I said to Promise—after the silence seemed to extend itself like a nasty form of punishment. I looked at her as I said this, and there was something in the way she returned my gaze that made me think *she* was angry.

Bob and I have our good days, I said. Days when this setup seems to take on something of secondary significance. But today—

Evan, Promise said—holding up a hand, and looking at Bob.

Hello, he finally said. It's good to meet you, Promise.

It's good to meet you, Bob.

And now can you help me to get out of here? Or are you crazy, too?

And there I stood, watching the two of them begin their dance. They no longer needed me. Thrust into the role of Cupid with nothing but time on his hands, I realized that it was long past dinner. I'd been too busy playing with my gun. No wonder Bob was grumpy.

Bob, Promise said—in a soothing tone. Could you give us a minute or two? We'll be right back.

With a little scrunch of her nose, she delivered these words in the voice of an anchor before a commercial break.

— —

Of course, I said. Speak your mind.

Evan, this is a fucking mess.

Promise and I were sitting at the kitchen table, and for some reason we were almost whispering.

Are you surprised?

Surprised? Promise said—shaking her head. Yes. *Yes*. I mean, seriously, Evan, I did suspect. A little maybe, but I thought it was a book.

A book?

You were writing a *book*, remember? About a guy in your basement. Sure I wondered a little, but in the back of my mind I kept saying to myself, No, he's not *that* crazy.

You wanted to see the basement, I whispered. You kept asking to see the basement.

She looked at me and said nothing. And what more could *I* say? I could've asked her to explain further, but I already knew the gist of what she was thinking. In that way, Promise had become a mirror. And what did I see? A blemish, a sore, an abscess. Maybe the wound got covered with a Band-Aid, but did that really help? You imagine you're an artist and you nurse it—the wound, the weakness—into a story or a novel; but in the end, minus success, it just oozes unseemly ambition.

A moment later Promise slowly shook her head, laughed; and then, her head thrown back, she screamed at the top of her lungs. So much for whispering. It scared the hell out of me. A wild shriek—like something coming out of a soccer player after a goal. For a moment I worried that she was hurt, physically, or that she was calling for help.

What a pretty kettle of fish, she said—shaking her head. What a fucking mess. You *are* a genius, Evan. But you're crazy. It's brilliant, the whole setup. It's so *you*. It's dawning on me. How right this is for you. I've been thinking about you for over a month now, trying to figure out who Evan Ulmer is, who he might be in a slightly different world, and all the while the answer has been right under my fucking nose.

What has?

You.

Promise was crying now — silently. I hadn't seen it coming, and I doubt she had either. Suddenly there were tears everywhere, in an arbitrary pattern of rivulets running down her face. They appeared at the corners of her eyes, pushed from the ducts one by one, in a queue of sorrow. Over what? And, as usually happens when someone starts crying, I found myself wanting to cry, too — either out of sympathy or envy.

OK, so let's think about this, Promise said — wiping the tears away with the sleeve of her brown dress. Partnow knows your name, right?

Yes.

He knows this is Sandhurst. You didn't blindfold him, getting him here?

No, he drove, I said — sheepishly, shrugging, feeling like such an amateur.

So, OK, then we're flat out of options.

You mean *I'm* out of options.

He knows who you are, she said, and so you can't just return him to his office, let him go, say you're sorry and move on.

I could kill him —

Oh yeah, right, she said — wiping her nose again. That's a good idea.

I know, I'm not the killer type. Plus, I like Bob.

Are you the kidnapping type?

Yes, I said, I guess so.

So you could become, you know, the penitent type. You let Robert Partnow go. You call the police —

Aren't you an accomplice?

Not yet.

No, you're the heroine, I said — without really thinking. Smiling, and then restraining that smile, I reached out and took her hand in mine.

You explain the situation, she said, and hope for the best.

I looked into Promise's eyes, squeezed her hand, and thought of hope—the concept—now so closely associated in my mind with this twenty-five-year-old whose cheeks were stained with the salty residue of tears. It wasn't the same as *feeling* hope, but it was in the neighborhood.

The best?

A reasonable prison sentence, she said.

Would you visit me? In prison?

Of course I'd visit you, she said.

Do you think I'm crazy?

For asking if I'd visit?

For abducting Bob Partnow, I said.

Yes, she said—almost screaming the word, as though I'd finally given her the chance. I mean, Evan, we're all a little crazy. But you went way over the line instead of nudging up to it. I mean, I knew about the Robert Partnow case. I read about it in *People.* I saw something on television about it. Naturally I thought about what the kidnapper would be like. What kind of scary person would do such a thing? And so if you'd told me that one day, *this* day, I'd be sitting here with the kidnapper—

Me.

Yes, you. And that I *wouldn't* be afraid. I'd tell you that you were—

Crazy, I said—finishing her sentence, then reaching into my jacket and retrieving the Magnum, the Colt Python.

My god, Evan.

You thought I made that up too? I said—sliding the gun across the table.

Can I?

Of course.

Slowly, Promise reached and took the gun in her hand. Holding it, she seemed uncomfortable; and I immediately recognized this as the way I'd once felt—as though holding a gun was itself a crime, a fudging of personal ethics.

You need to let me handle this, Promise said—looking down,

tapping her foot on the kitchen linoleum, the gun still in her hand.

What are you going to do?

Are there bullets in here? Promise said—staring at it.

No, I said.

We're probably going to need to call the police, she said. You realize that.

Yes. Of course. Before we do that, before we call the police, can I go down and talk with Bob again? I mean, you can come too. Just for a minute?

Promise looked up at me without expression. A bit of hair hung in her face. And even though, right then, she continued to hold the gun awkwardly—like it was a fork or a cell phone—she seemed different. In one single, blazing moment there had been a shift in our relationship, and now there was something almost pitiful about my request—*Just for a minute?*—as though all I had was feeble rhetoric with which to get what I wanted. Holding a firearm, Promise could do whatever she wanted to do. It was undeniable—the gun had increased her options, her range of response. She was scaring me.

I don't see why not, she said.

I don't see why not. It's embarrassing to say this, but it was easily the sexiest thing Promise had ever said to me. She looked me directly in the eye, and I had no idea what she might say; and then she said—quickly, emphatically—*I don't see why not.* And yes, of course it had to do with the fact that she was holding a gun.

I couldn't have predicted it, but I had an erection. Under the table, out of view, in my pants. I had a boner, and I was going to prison, and at that moment I felt split—my life headed, all of a sudden, in two very different directions.

— —

Bob was watching television. I took this as a sign that things had probably gone too far. Was this really the time to be watching television—after the national news, short of prime time, after having met Promise and contemplated the possibility of release?

Evan's decided to inform the police of your whereabouts, Promise said.

That's good news, Bob said—turning off the television.

Really, Bob, I said. Truly.

OK, I believe you, he said—giving me a strange smile.

And then, as he looked over and saw the gun in Promise's hand, I watched his face dissolve. You don't realize the way a face is constantly maintained, held up as though with invisible strings, until you see one—confronted with the unexpected—lose itself.

A gun, Promise said—seeing the look on Bob's face; and she pointed it vaguely in the direction of the television, her finger now on the trigger. She seemed more comfortable with it—not quite an old pro, but certainly an amateur with a steep learning curve.

You told me there wasn't any gun.

Yes, I said. I apologize, Bob. We were in the prevarication phase, if you remember. Also I wanted to put you at ease, if that's any consolation. OK, no, I suppose it isn't. But I thought it best not to completely burn my bridges.

And why does she have the gun?

She? Promise said. That's me you're talking about, and I have the gun because Evan gave me the gun.

It looks like she's in charge, I said—shrugging, trying to make light of our mutual predicament.

You've called the police? Bob asked.

Not yet, Promise said. Is there anything else you'd like to say, Evan?

Oh god, I said—clearing my throat, feeling the sudden pinch of time, flashing back to a wedding toast I once gave, reluctantly, for a second cousin. There are so many things I'd like to say. But I feel like I'm on my deathbed here.

Nobody's dying, Promise said—as though, with the gun in her hand, she'd know.

First off, you've been an ideal abductee, Bob, you really have. Let's begin there. I don't have a lot of experience with this, but it just seems to me it could've been a lot worse. I mean, from *my* perspective. And I appreciate your reading my manuscript. And your comments, of course. Your encouragement. And I hope that I haven't screwed up your life too much. I know the hard part is ahead of you. The girls, your daughters. Plus Claudia and Lloyd and the mess of all of that. I'm sorry, I don't mean *mess* to make it sound—

He knows what you mean, Promise said.

You do?

Yes, Bob said.

Thanks, I said.

Thank *you*, he said—and I didn't know whether he was kidding, making a joke, or being dead serious. Somehow, in the surreal swirl of things, what with the vertigo I was now experiencing, I couldn't trust myself to make these distinctions. Things were going too fast, a drama was unfolding; I felt as though I'd just run into Nicole Kidman at the market—my shoes covered in Thousand Island dressing, my heart in my throat. Except that at this moment I was watching the arc of my own demise.

Do you have the key to the lock here? Promise said—motioning with the gun toward the heavy, solid brass lock on the door to Bob's cage.

Shouldn't we call the police first? I asked—but even as I said this, I was digging into the pocket of my jeans. I tossed the key ring to Promise. The gun in one hand, she made the catch with the other.

I'm going to let Bob out, she said. And I'm going to ask you, Evan, to go inside.

Inside?

Bear with me, Evan. It's really for the best.

Shouldn't we wait for the police? I asked.

We *are* waiting for the police, she said.

I looked at Bob, but he was already in motion—grabbing his leather satchel off the top of the refrigerator.

— ∙ —

Are you in a hurry? Promise asked.

How do you mean? Bob said—hopping on one foot, pulling on his second zippered boot with a bit of trouble. He'd come out of the cage in his stocking feet, carrying the shoes. Apparently he *was* in a hurry, or at least it seemed that way to me. (I've always been sensitive to the whole idea of quick departure.) Bob did look good in his old suit pants—he had a little more space around the middle. I watched with pride as he reworked the belt, inserted the buckle into the next hole without much effort.

I was thinking, Promise said. What if I don't call the police?

I'll call the police, Bob said.

What if right now no one calls the police? she said to Bob. That's what I meant. I thought maybe you might want to stick around.

Stick around? *Here?*

Now that Evan's on the inside. Locked up and all. I mean, there's no danger. And so there's no hurry, right? Or is there?

Promise walked over to the door of the cage, put the gun under her arm, and used both hands to close the heavy lock. Watching her, I realized I hadn't noticed that she hadn't already locked it; but once I heard the sound, it felt like something inside me was slamming shut—yet another door to my heart.

And anyway, why not do it *your* way? she asked.

What are you talking about? Bob said—adjusting the satchel on his shoulder and staring at me; he was talking to Promise, but looking at me in my new residence. Are you saying I'm going to have to *walk* to a police station?

You don't have to do anything, Promise said. I just thought, OK, it's been a bad chapter in your life, and so why not fashion the end of it yourself? I don't know. Maybe I'm wrong. But, if I call the police, do you think there *isn't* going to be an onslaught of media, a feeding frenzy? You think a couple of Johnny Laws are going to drive over here in a squad car and quietly whisk you back to Manhattan?

I leaned into the fence with one shoulder. I was watching the two of them, thinking of *fashion*—the word—and how I'd never probably used it as a verb in my entire life; and thinking that suddenly I had become an afterthought, a voiceless child, a mute prisoner looking out at my two keepers without even the slenderest of hopes. I had no idea what Promise was up to, but I *was* impressed.

You don't know this, I said, but Bob used to be a writer.

Visibly startled, the two of them stared at me as though—monkey in cage, fluke of evolution—I'd just opened my mouth and spoken the King's English.

A long time ago, I said.

Well, maybe the writer's desire to control fate never completely goes away, Promise said—her tone almost professorial.

And then Bob was staring at me again, and with some suspicion, it seemed—or was he trying to figure out what *I* was thinking? I tried to smile, but my smile soon wilted, and Bob's eyes glazed over and he began nodding as though some notion inside his head had just then been confirmed.

I wouldn't mind looking around a little, he said—turning to Promise.

I could give you a tour, she said.

What I *need* is the gun, Bob said.

The gun? Promise said.

Yes, he said—pointing a finger at it.

Mr. Partnow, she said—pointing it back at him, returning the rudeness of his impertinent finger—here's a question for you. Are you planning on pressing charges?

I'm not feeling particularly comfortable, that's what I'm saying. I don't know you. I've never met you before. And you're sort of pointing a gun at me.

Sort of?

Her uncle knows you, Bob, I said. What's his name, Promise?

That doesn't matter, she said—her eyes on Bob.

Who? he asked. What's his name?

Nathaniel Reed, she said—and Bob nodded his head and gave a brief smile. You went to college with him.

It's true, Bob said—extending his hand toward the gun.

Are you going to hurt Evan?

Evan? he said. Hurt Evan? No. With the gun? No. Me, I couldn't shoot a squirrel on a dare. Maybe I reject writers, but I don't *shoot* them.

So Evan, Promise said—talking out of the side of her mouth, her eyes never leaving Bob's—do you have thoughts about the gun?

It's a beautiful weapon, I said—shrugging. More dangerous in fantasy than in fact. But also much heavier than you might think, Bob.

And, as though my words released her from her quandary, Promise handed Bob the gun. Watching this transaction, I couldn't help thinking of her as a polite first-grader who'd just learned the proper way to hand over a pair of scissors. *It's safer that way, kids.* She gave him the weapon butt first—and so, at least for a moment, the gun was pointed directly at her.

And the key, Bob said. I need that, too.

.

10

For most kids, being grounded meant you couldn't leave the house, couldn't get together with your buddies. My father must've known I wasn't flush with friends, and so when he grounded me I was locked alone in my bedroom for the day, the week, whatever. Not actually locked, of course. I had permission to go to the bathroom, I did my household chores, sat in the dining room and ate my dinner and listened to my father's tales of workplace woe. But mostly I was limited to my room.

My father's mistake was to assume that I ever wanted to leave my room. Yes, there was an initial stretch of boredom. But sooner or later I'd find a pen or pencil and transport myself—zooming off somewhere in my imagination. Other children might've sat there biting the bullet or playing games of solitaire or closing their eyes and using their minds to imagine a better world. For me, escape always required a pen or pencil.

When I was young, I mostly drew pictures—often representations of my parents, with tiny horns or stunted tails or other residual signs of what I then took to be their true natures. In a neat reversal, they were usually cooped up in some crudely rendered zoo, the bars of which I drew, meticulously, with my favorite wooden ruler. But as I got a little older, I gave up on pictures and turned to the written word. I made up stories, manipulating circumstance with narrative flights of imagination. And my pleasure always came from the feeling that I was subverting my father's will, getting away with something.

YOU THINK YOU KNOW someone. And on the strength of that knowledge you bow your head and shuffle behind chain-link of your own making; you turn your home over to some wandering editor who isn't quite ready to resume his regular life; and suddenly the girl with the mouth to die for, the one to whom you've revealed your every secret—she becomes a virtual stranger.

Not that any of this came as a huge surprise. I'd always been the dupe as far back as I can remember. Even those few occasions when I managed to believe in myself—weren't they evidence enough of a tendency toward belief at any cost?

These bad thoughts tore through my mind in the first few hours of detention. I have to admit that I was feeling sorry for myself, having assumed the role of fall guy in someone else's tale of triumph. But then I began to question my assumptions. I mean, how was I to know what Promise was thinking? What if she was trying to protect me from myself, as it were? Promise may have been wrong—having failed to see how willing I was to relinquish control of my own abduction scenario—but could you blame her for playing it safe?

Those and many other questions came to the fore, questions about my not-so-far-off future. Would Promise move to a squalid prison town and while away her late twenties until she realized that there were plenty of romantic possibilities back in Manhattan, all of them preferable? Would I still get an occasional call on the prison telephone? Would she send Christmas cards with pictures of the children?

— —

I'm sorry.

You're sorry, I said. I'm the sorry one.

I had to, Promise said—and she looked up at the ceiling,

presumably in the direction of Bob, who was still upstairs and doing what?

Serves me right being in here, I said.

No, it doesn't, she said—in a flat tone, from the other side of the
fence. There's nothing right or wrong about it.

A taste of my own medicine.

It won't be forever, she said.

I looked at Promise and saw annoyance on her face. Her words
were meant to offer solace, but her pained eyes and the frown that
shot across her forehead told a different story. An hour earlier, she'd
seemed so animated in talking strategy at the kitchen table; now she
looked exhausted, her brown dress wrinkled, her eyes weary. Was it
me? Was it the thought of going upstairs and making sure that Bob
hadn't taken his gun, his key, and fled south on the Metro-North?

It's driving me crazy, there's not one pencil or pen in this whole
damn place, I said—lowering myself to one knee, dipping my head
under the bunk bed. I should've known. Bob, the editor. Bob, the
ex-writer.

You feel like writing? Promise said. Right now?

On hands and knees, I looked up at her and cleared my throat. I
was embarrassed by the urge, but there it was. And she didn't seem
to mind; in fact, she found a few yellow pencils, blunted but not beyond usefulness, at the base of the stairs, and jabbed them through
the fence, along with a rolled-up pad of yellow paper.

I know this isn't going to be easy for you, she said. But I think I
need to leave now.

Leave?

Just for a while. Just for the night.

OK.

I don't know, she said—looking past me, squinting and gazing
off into the distance. I talked to Bob about it, and I think it's the
right thing to do. I'll go home and—

What *do* you and Bob talk about? I asked—thinking of the hours
that had already passed.

I'll go home, try to get a good night's sleep, Promise said. Bob? He's trying to put the pieces together.

What pieces?

And I'm trying to help him. Anyway, I'll be back tomorrow. It's best, I think, for you and Bob to be alone.

What if—

And don't worry about Bob. He's—

I waited for Promise to finish, but suddenly her face froze.

What? I said. What?

God, I just had an idea.

About—

It's stupid, she said. Something just dawned on me. About my novel. Just an idea. I'm sorry, Evan. Forget it. Sorry to bring it up.

That's OK.

I've got the itch, too, I guess, she said—laughing, wiggling the fingers of both hands, as though typing. Anyway, Bob's upstairs. Last I saw, he was standing there in the hallway. Mesmerized, it looked like, by your father's diploma.

Without another word, Promise trudged up the stairs, thoughts of her novel no doubt foremost in her mind. And I stood there, motionless, my nose up against the fence, and wondered what to make of this, her first visit since she'd lured me into the cage. And when would she visit next?

Given the situation, was it insensitive of her to bring up her own novel? In my case, it was understandable—after all, I was trying to pass the time and make something of my circumstances. What was Promise's excuse? Then again, wasn't she exhibiting the tenacity she'd taught me, by example, day after day at the library—the ability to write no matter what the situation? Only writers understand the ruthlessness with which anything and everything, at any moment, could be twisted, turned, and translated into words. We were like magicians who couldn't resist fiddling with the change in our pockets, making coins disappear with or without an audience.

After Promise left—and yes, maybe to escape even the thought of her—I lay on my new bunk bed, on the sniffling edge of weeping, and moved the pencil across the paper like a zombie, like a crazed poet. I scribbled and scribbled. To be writing on anything other than the pages of my green notebooks—it felt promiscuous. I'd always used yellow pads for grocery lists.

— —

So what's it going to be? *Nightline? Letterman?*

I wasn't sure how to respond to Bob's first words after coming down the stairs and sitting down in the chair on *his* side of the fence. I appreciated the continuity—another night, another programming decision—but I was suspicious of his tone.

Not sure I'm in the mood, I said—sitting up on the bed, ducking to avoid hitting my head on the upper bunk.

What have you been doing?

What have *you* been doing?

I asked first, he said.

I've been writing, working on the novel, the manuscript. Finishing up, writing the last chapters. Working the narrative toward the inevitable moment of punishment. And wondering what you were up to, what you were thinking up there.

Yes, of course, Bob said, what's crime without punishment? I didn't know you were so close.

Close?

To finishing, he said. The novel. You're close?

Yes. I've had a sudden burst of—

Creative energy.

I wouldn't call it that, I said—cringing, covertly, at the jargon. But yes, something. I've written another chapter.

Any surprises?

That's actually a problem. Punishment has a way of playing out like a foregone conclusion.

Yes, Bob said, and it's kind of a downer. I mean, from an editor's point of view. Things getting worse and not better.

What about you? I said — directing my eyes toward the chocolate-colored insulation and what lay above it. Any surprises your way?

Your place is kind of spare.

You mean downstairs, I said. The living room.

I mean everywhere. I knew you didn't have a lot of things, but I just thought there might be more —

Furniture.

Yes. And books.

I'm not a collector of books, I said. I tend to get them from libraries. Or I buy and then sell after I've read them. My parents were never keen on owning books.

Is that your parents in that picture in the hallway?

Upstairs? Yes. Harold and Kay.

They look grim.

They're dead and so they have every reason to be grim, I said.

And then I realized I'd never spoken much to Bob about my parents, even though we'd talked a lot about his. This might've been the first I'd told him that they were no longer alive. (I had a way of speaking about them as though they were still breathing down my neck.) Of course, he'd read about them in a fictional context, but that was different.

— · —

Your bed is too soft, Bob said the next morning — standing there, stretching, yawning, twisting his upper torso right, then left. I slept sporadically. You want some breakfast?

I guess a bowl of cereal wouldn't hurt. Grape Nuts.

Whole milk? Nonfat milk?

Nonfat, I said.

I realize I've never shared a breakfast with you. I don't know what you eat.

So when's Promise showing up?

Lunchtime, Bob said — looking at his watch. By the way, Evan, could you do me a favor and hand me that manuscript over there?

I followed Bob's gaze and saw the typed copy of my novel sitting where I'd left it the night before, next to the bunk beds. I'd stayed up far too late — checking over the manuscript, shortening pencils, writing new scenes on my yellow pad, worrying over narrative coherence.

I'd like to see it again, he said.

I walked it over and wedged it, in three rolled-up installments, through the chain-link fence. Bob sat down and aligned the pages of the manuscript in his lap.

This isn't your only copy, is it?

You mean—

Hard copy, printed copy. Doesn't Promise have one?

Promise hasn't read my book, I said.

You're kidding. Not a word?

No.

You two share only bodies? Bob said — giving me a crooked smile that struck me as uncharacteristically lascivious. By the way, I ran across a few of your notebooks in the kitchen. The green notebooks. And up in the bedroom closet, too, next to the porno. That's quite a collection you've got there.

Nothing I'm proud of, I said.

I meant the collection of notebooks, Bob said.

Those? Yeah, well, years of—

How many do you think you have total?

I've been writing since I was a kid, I said. If nothing else, failure tends to add up. Accumulate.

It's impressive, Bob said — nodding. All that labor.

— —

Promise walked up to the fence, where I was standing, and brought her face close to the chain-link. I thought she was going to whisper something to me — a secret between us, to be kept from Bob, who was standing a few feet away. Instead she pursed her lips and offered a kiss. As it turned out, the diamond was the perfect size for four lips—a mutual orifice, as it were. It was a very quick kiss, almost perfunctory; but I took it, like a crumb dropped into a beggar's hand, and realized how much I'd needed that kiss, however paltry or sisterly or whatever it was. At certain times, nothing seems so much a sacrament, an avowal of things unchanging, as a kiss.

I brought sandwiches, Promise said—holding up a brown paper bag. Can we turn off the television?

Bob and I had been watching *Jenny Jones*—a bad habit of ours dating back to a few days before we'd switched places. (Typically, we'd held to the upper echelon of talk shows. *Montel* became our best attempt at a dividing line, a standard of mediocrity.) It was obviously a rerun—pretty much everyone in the studio audience was in Halloween attire. In a platinum blonde wig, Jenny was a fudged Marilyn Monroe without the bust, asking the couple on stage in breathy tones to explain how the cheating had begun. It had begun, it seemed, in Cleveland.

I clicked off the TV. Bob made a polite motion toward the single chair, but Promise shook her head. And so Bob sat down himself, turning the chair backwards, straddling it like some world-weary detective in charge of the investigation.

So how are things? Promise asked.

Neither of us answered at first. I cleared my throat. I was waiting for Bob, and he must've been waiting for me. I don't know about Bob, but I felt awkward and strangely deferential.

Bob's been upstairs a lot, I said.

I've been getting to know Evan. Trying on his shoes, so to speak.

And is it working? Promise asked him.

More or less, he said.

Lunch? she said—shaking the bag, still in her hand.

Is *what* working? I said—looking from Promise to Bob, and then down at his shoes, which were in fact his own. Black boots, zippered. There was a conspiratorial silence between the two of them,

I couldn't help thinking; they weren't so much waiting for the other to speak, it seemed, as waiting for my question to be whisked away by friendly spirits.

I don't know what I was expecting. Fireworks? An educational seminar, a three-way discussion on abduction and its psychological ramifications in the minds of victims and perpetrators? Some sense of what in the hell was going on, or some indication that everyone was confused—or was it just me?

What about you, Evan? Promise asked—unrolling the top of the paper bag. What have you been doing?

Me? Writing like a banshee. And worrying, more or less, about what Bob's doing when he's not down here.

— —

Is there a reason you keep playing with the gun?

Do I keep playing with the gun? Bob said—looking down at the weapon as though he'd just then noticed its existence.

Yes. Every time you come down here.

Does it scare you?

A little, I said. Mostly it makes me wonder if that's what you want.

To scare you? No, it's not at the top of my list.

What *is* at the top of your list?

Bob gazed upward, toward the ceiling, and then covered his eyes with the hand that wasn't holding the gun. He was thinking—or was he simply trying to give that impression? Bob was becoming more enigmatic with each visit.

I'm not an impulsive man, he finally said. Did you know that about me?

I didn't know that, I said—not quite telling the truth.

I'm not.

What about Lloyd?

Lloyd? Bob said—frowning. I knew Lloyd for two years before

I reached across the table at Dean & DeLuca and touched his forearm. Just because you sleep with a man doesn't mean you're impulsive.

But you were married.

Getting married, Bob said—nodding. Yes, that's probably the most impulsive thing I've ever done. Anyway, what's at the top of my list? Figuring out what to do. What to do *now*. What to do *next*.

About me, you mean.

You, Evan? No. Really, you're the least of my concerns. And I keep telling myself, *Now don't be impulsive*. It's odd that way. I've been talking to myself. A lot. And I've been doing a little scheming.

About—

My vocation, he said.

—•—

It would've been nice to have the typed manuscript in front of me, to check for continuity. (I thought about asking Bob if I could see it again, but—flattered he was taking another look—I didn't want to disturb him.) Nonetheless, I kept writing on the yellow pad, and with the same urgency. I was writing about the loss of love, about physical separation, the hellish grind of daily life behind bars— using present circumstance as inspirational grist. I was worrying, too, whether the ending was getting too sentimental, almost soppy. Was I just feeling sorry for myself?

When I wasn't writing, I was more or less twiddling my thumbs. It was then that I felt most lonely—like a dog waiting for one of its masters to walk through the door. It was one thing to write about being alone, about suffering the indignity of prison life and not knowing the next time you'd see your girl; it was another thing altogether to while away the hours of captivity.

Once or twice, to pass the time, I leafed through Bob's collection of articles about himself. I thought this might make me feel better. But, in fact, the articles upset me—the shallow sensationalistic prose and the way I found myself described as a loser with a low threshold for the everyday frustrations of a career as a middling writer. It wasn't that I entirely disagreed with the portrayal. It was worse than that.

— —

My novel? she said. It's going nowhere. Not at the moment.

Standing there on the other side of the fence, Promise was still wearing her sunglasses. I wanted her to take them off. I wanted her to sit down and spend some time. I wanted her to walk over and kiss me through the fence.

I'm not complaining.

You can complain.

I guess I *am* complaining, she said—bowing her head. I'm just feeling overwhelmed.

Overwhelmed? I said—thinking of myself, sleeping on a bunk bed, dreaming of kissing my loved one through a makeshift glory hole.

I'm like a hall monitor here, Promise said—waving her hand in front of her, wiping an imaginary blackboard. I've got you here, on the inside, looking very unhappy in spite of your spurt of writing. And I've got Bob upstairs. And it's talk, talk, talk. He's quite a talker.

Bob?

He's really a pretty sweet guy, but he's been moaning about his headaches, demanding groceries.

It's only been a day, I said.

Almost two. Anyway, I'm sorry, Evan, I shouldn't complain. It's not like I don't have *time* to write. I do. But it's different now. I can't seem to *see* you. Evan Ulmer, who *is* he? Every time I ask myself that question, I just see *you. Here.* Looking sad. And I end up wanting to help you, Evan, I do. Even if you're an idiot for having done what you've done.

I know, I said.

I can't seem to think of you as anything other than *you*.

I know the feeling, I said.

Doesn't it feel humid down here, Promise said—waving a hand in front of her face. A little musty?

Are you going to let me out?

Evan, you know I don't have the key.

You seem to have a lot of influence over Bob.

Let's hope so.

You could cut the chain-link fence, I said. I could tell you where the wire cutters are.

The situation is in Bob's hands right now, Promise said—and she seemed to cringe slightly in saying this. And it's really best to stick to the deal.

Deal? I said. What deal?

— —

Evan, Bob said, you've got that pencil in your hand every time I come down here. Do you sleep with it?

I'd be a happier person if I did, I said.

You must be getting close.

Close?

To finishing your novel, he said. Congratulations.

Did you sleep with Promise?

What?

Upstairs. In my bed.

Last night?

Any night.

Evan, Bob said, you're not thinking straight. And I know, I know how it works. Captivity has consequences. It can fry the brain if you let it.

I just thought I'd ask, I said—trying to avoid the look of someone begging for a little peace of mind.

You think I'd get released from my kidnapping, Bob said, and then turn around and fuck the girl who was fucking the kidnapper?

We never—

She's not my type, Evan.

— —

Two days and still I refused to give myself a sponge bath. I also refused to ask for food, even though Bob had been spotty with meals. Already he'd fallen into a habit of slipping Almond Joys through the fence, as if these passed for sustenance. (I knew how he'd gotten them. Promise had done a little shopping, and obviously without an eye toward denial.) I pleaded for patience from my bladder, going into the Porta-Potty reluctantly, latching the door each time for no particular reason. I stared at the treadmill and not once did it occur to me to climb aboard. I was a resistant prisoner, far less amenable than Bob had ever been.

Meanwhile, I was finding it difficult to think of Promise as anyone other than my keeper. Maybe Bob was the driving force behind my captivity, but Promise seemed to be the one steering the boat. Better Promise than Bob, maybe; but still it made me worry. And it would've been nice if Promise had chosen to lock herself inside with me. Certainly kissing would've been better without the impediment of chain-link. But she didn't deserve punishment; she'd done nothing wrong—not yet, at least.

If it hadn't been for the novel, the idea of finishing it, I don't know how I would've made it through those first long hours of detention.

— —

There's something wrong with you.

With *me*? Bob said.

A person gets abducted and then gets free, and then he sticks around?

I'm not sticking around.

What do you call this? I asked—my arms outstretched, plaintively, from my side of the fence.

Don't worry, he said, I'm leaving. Sooner than you might think.

I'm not talking about how *long* you plan to stay. I'm talking about staying at all. What kind of person gets free and then stays? OK, so I'm the crazy fuck who pulled you off a Manhattan street, but what kind of victim spends a night at the scene of the crime? *Two* nights.

You have a limited imagination, he said. That may be your biggest problem.

What does that mean?

— —

It's just—

It's just what, Evan?

You've always been so candid. I can't remember you ever *not* answering a question.

I can't remember you ever asking me *that* kind of question, Promise said.

It's just a question.

No it isn't.

Maybe it's because I'm here, in this cage, I said—looking around, experiencing for a moment the perils of guessing at my own psychology. I'm alone here. And we haven't seen a lot of each other. And—

Promise and I stood there for a moment, on either side of the fence—like two kids at a playground, I couldn't help thinking. And I waited for her to say something. Was she waiting for me, too? I felt that nagging tickle at the back of my throat, but I resisted it.

You still want me to answer your question, don't you?

Yes, I said—shrugging, that sheepish feeling coming over me.

No.

No?

No. That's my answer.

I'm sorry, I said. I am. For asking. It just seemed—

It just seemed like I was fucking Bob?

I looked at her, and Promise looked at me. And that word, *fucking*—coming out of her mouth, the same one I'd kissed—it tore at some seam running down the middle of me. I don't know why, but it did.

— —

Despite my unhappiness at being held against my will, it was getting easier to write. For once, I was sailing with a tailwind. Romance, confinement, punishment—the pieces were coming together, the protagonist's contrite epiphany written with Bob's criteria of salability in mind. (Some worry—were things getting too weepy?) Even though I was tiring of the stench of my own body, and fantasizing about food with something other than corn syrup as primary ingredient, I was feeling, for once, like a writer.

No, Bob wouldn't be visiting me in whatever prison I eventually landed in. And he wouldn't be any help in getting the book published. And yes, that was a little disheartening; it wasn't easy to meet editors, let alone have their undivided attention for a few weeks to convince them of your merits. But Bob's assessment of the unfinished manuscript continued to spur me on—his positive words replaying in my mind like a loopy reel of encouragement. I felt pitiful in wheeling out these words—*very good, impressive*—like some huge billboard dedicated to myself. But then, what choice does a nervous author have?

— —

I'm down here in this cage, I said, and you're up there, at least most of the time, when you're not down here watching television, and—

What's your question, Evan?

How long is this going to go on?

I don't know, Bob said—scrunching up his shoulders. Should I?

I feel like you're playing games, Bob.

Editors aren't supposed to?

You're not my editor, I said.

Exactly, he said. And who knows, maybe I'm nobody's. Maybe my days of reading are over.

My manuscript? I asked—because I couldn't help myself. Are you still rereading it?

Your *manuscript,* Bob said—clearly enunciating the three syllables. Isn't that a strange word? Basically my whole adult life has been taken up with that word.

I finished, I said—holding up the yellow pad, holding back a smile.

I was going to ask about that. Can I see?

It's in longhand. And my penmanship—

With the calm of an editor, making a joke of his insistence, Bob jutted a hand toward the fence and looked the other way. Obligingly, I rolled up the yellow pages and scooted them through the fence.

As for the *rest* of the manuscript, Bob said, it's gone.

Gone?

Sorry, he said. I had to destroy it. I had a little fire upstairs in the living room.

A fire?

Yes, a fire.

You burned it? I said—and in the pit of my stomach, I felt a sickening lift, as though some demon had snatched my bowels and yanked *up*. You *didn't* burn it.

Actually, Evan, I did.

You *burned* it?

It wasn't like a book-burning, if that's what you mean. No liturgy, no pyre. I just tossed it in the fire. And also the green notebooks.

The notebooks? I said—suddenly seeing their number, their history, the times I'd taken them with me into coffee shops, bus terminals, dark bars in dangerous neighborhoods. Never, not once, had I lost or misplaced one.

Listen, Evan, it's not as though your best work is behind you.

My fucking notebooks? I yelled.

And also the computer hard drive. That went into the fire too. Took a hammer to it first, just in case.

I heard the pounding, I said—more to myself than Bob, and suddenly the vague, faraway sound from earlier in the day came back to me. That hammer might as well have been landing on my head. *Wham, wham, wham.* With each new mention of an archival mode—*manuscript, notebooks, hard drive*—I realized that, yes, there was yet another way of salvaging at least a few of my words, my mental meanderings. But now everything was gone. *Gone.* There was nowhere left to find the words, other than in my head—and my head was *throbbing.* I thought I was going to throw up.

I knew this would upset you, Bob said, but I had no choice.

I had no choice, I said—tasting bile. Isn't that what Jeffrey Dahmer said?

When?

What do you mean *when?* Just before he stuck his fork into another piece of young-boy ass. Do you have any fucking idea—

I'm especially sorry about the computer, Bob said. That memoir you began about your Wisconsin childhood. You know, growing up in a hotbed of political and religious conservatism. Blah blah blah. And those long e-mail exchanges with strangers.

They weren't *strangers.*

Some of it was very—

Very *what?* I said—clearing my throat, making room for judgment.

Touching.

II

◂O▸

As far back as I can remember, I've thought of writers as vessels, as go-betweens. That's what it feels like, after all—making things up, listening to strange voices, transcribing the demons, and forever feeling as though your mind is a straw sucking up bits of reality.

Promise and I always agreed on this—the self-contained writer, standing like some confident puppeteer above the fray, was pure myth. (Kafka certainly didn't alter this opinion; his diaries, the ones Promise carried to the library, gave him away as the sad fuckup he was.) There's no escaping the fray. Orchestrate a little, channel a few voices, stare in bewilderment at what you've managed to scribble on the page, and wipe that sweat from your brow. Declare yourself a lucky son of a bitch if you get anything down on paper.

All of it happens, if it happens, in spite of you, with barely a polite nod to any of your so-called mysterious powers. It's not a rabbit pulled from a hat—more a cat out of the bag.

D ID ANYONE CALL the police? I asked.

Promise and I were in my kitchen, standing on either side of the stove. I'd just poured her a martini because she asked for one. I wasn't in the mood for wooziness myself; since Bob's cruel announcement, I hadn't *stopped* feeling light-headed.

Promise nibbled at the edge of the glass—making a rude sound, like a child with a straw—and then laughed. Was she laughing at herself? At me?

Am I being stupid?

No, she said—with a pitying frown. Not at all. I can see, Evan. You assumed they were just taking their time.

Something about Promise's answer, her practiced patience, annoyed me. It hadn't been *that* long since she'd opened the door to the cage and informed me of Bob's departure; and she'd never said anything about the police *not* showing up, and so how was I to know?

No police, Promise said. Nope. And you're not going to prison.

What does that mean?

It means you're not going to prison.

— —

What had I expected? An intact manuscript, a gleaming hard drive, my green notebooks stacked neatly behind the heavy mesh curtain? Of course not. But down on my hands and knees, staring into the fireplace, I expected at least to see evidence of a fire—ashes, papery debris. Instead, I found nothing.

Was this a sign that the fire had been a hoax, a cruel lie? If the fireplace hadn't been so obviously swept clean of debris, I might've taken it as a good omen; I might've even entertained fantasies of reprieve—gone scurrying room to room, searching for the manuscript. But the fireplace, spotless inside and out, suggested only a houseguest who meticulously removed all traces of his stay. Everything was *too* clean.

Minutes later, walking into my bedroom, I discovered that all traces *hadn't* been removed. Demurely, poised on my pillow was the gun; a few inches away, on the smoothed bedspread, there was a thick, clear plastic bag, with a red twist tie securing its contents. Inside? Something gray, black, white—a mound of ashes. I could also make out twisted bits of metal, some corkscrewed beyond recognition. My charred hard drive?

I picked it up, this bag, and held it in my hands like the remains of someone's cat.

—•—

It means you're not going to prison. Are you disappointed?

I thought—

It was either that or your book, Promise said—arms akimbo. One or the other. That was sort of the deal.

You think Bob isn't going to press charges?

He won't.

Come on, Promise.

I told him if he did, I'd personally sink an ax into his fucking heart. Plus, I'd claim he raped me. Wouldn't that make a mess of an already messy marriage? Anyway, he's already taken his revenge, Evan. He's not inclined to press charges.

He told you about Claudia?

We talked, she said. He's an OK guy. He's a little weird, and not overly fond of you.

What does *that* mean?

Listen, Evan, I know you're devastated, she said—yanking on one sleeve, shifting the martini glass as she worked herself out of her cardigan sweater. I'd be devastated, too. And angry. Anyone so much as *thought* of touching a novel of mine, I'd tear their eyes out with my fingernails.

And my notebooks, I said.

And your notebooks.

Was it really necessary?

As Promise considered my question, I saw she had on the Lycra top her mother had been wearing only a week before. Her nipples, mirror images of her mother's, fought against the fabric in a losing battle. At that moment this wasn't something I wanted to see.

Apparently it *was* necessary, Promise said. Or *he* felt it was. He wanted to get rid of all the traces. And let's face it, there was probably a little revenge in there, too. Like I said—

He's not particularly fond of me.

Exactly, she said. Look, Evan, I *am* sorry, but you're not going to prison. *And* you can write the book again.

For a moment I just stared at her. I thought of grabbing her cardigan sweater, shoving it into her hand, and turning her by the shoulders toward the foyer, toward the front door. *Out, out—you and your nipples and your perky optimism.*

This is worse than prison, I said. And I *can't* write the book again.

No, it isn't. And, of course, you can.

— —

It wasn't as though it had ever been a piece of cake. I mean, how many times had *I* considered burning it all, deleting every file, pouring acid on my hard drive, or feeding every page of everything I'd ever written to a ravenous paper shredder?

Still, as soon as they'd been taken away from me, I wanted them back—those poor lost words, now relegated to one of God's recycling bins. *Hey, they weren't so bad.* There must've been a few sentences worth saving. (Kafka thought his work was worthless and asked his best friend to burn it after he died; and now they stitch the K-man's name on baseball hats.) I felt the same way a son might feel after his parents have died and he realizes they weren't such awful parents, not really. Incapable of love, maybe, but who amongst us *is* capable?

In any case, after Bob left and I gave up searching for traces of my writing life, I sat around in a stupor for a couple of days. And did what? Nothing, absolutely nothing. I didn't watch television. I stood around for hours down in the basement—swinging open the door to the cage, swinging it closed. Over and over I tried to make sense of things. I closed my eyes and imagined I was asleep and about to wake up from a nightmare. And when I wasn't down in the basement, I wandered through the rest of the house in a daze, in my bathrobe and slippers. I consoled myself with chicken-noodle soup and saltines.

Promise stopped by twice that first week. The second time, she stayed for dinner and even spent the night. We talked a lot over fried dumplings and moo shu pork, and then we kissed in the kitchen—but how best to describe the failure of those kisses? Me? Stiff, self-conscious, as though someone was watching through the window, assessing the authenticity of this act of reciprocity. Promise? I have no idea. But I do know that our mouths searched in vain for a comfortable position. Our tongues were no longer swimming but drowning—inundated with spittle; and suddenly *saliva* was running through my mind as the word most likely running through hers.

That night, Promise ended up in my bed while I slept in Bob's bottom bunk down in the basement. It seemed like the right thing to do, even if it depressed the hell out of me. I dozed fitfully all night. In the morning, sausage sizzling in a fry pan wafted down the stairs and straight up my nose. It could've been a good, reassuring smell—domesticity to the rescue—but it wasn't. It stank of lard. Promise and I ate breakfast in a cloud of silence, accentuated by the humming refrigerator. And then she left.

Why had she chosen to stay over? Was it an act of kindness? Was she worried that I might use the gun against myself?

— —

Making it up, duping a reader into imagining that words on the page pass for reality—the whole enterprise now seemed both beyond my powers and a bit beneath me.

In the past, I might have felt inept on any given day, but it was a temporary affliction—just another bout of writer's block. I knew what it was to feel pitiful, to see my own fiction as a circle jerk of the imagination. I knew the way writing fiction could make you feel like a six-year-old moving little green plastic soldiers behind mounds of backyard dirt. In the past, I always waited a day or two for this bad feeling to dissipate. But this, now, seemed different.

Promise offered up her own prognosis. Optimistic as ever, she argued that the delusion I was really suffering under was that I'd never again suffer the *other,* necessary delusion—the one about being a writer. In the end, though, did it actually matter? My mother told me, back when I was a teenager, that I wasn't *really* unhappy, I only thought I was. But wasn't that as good a definition of unhappiness as any?

Promise said she thought I had a yearning for punishment. (A *hard-on*, in her cruel usage.) Otherwise, why didn't I appreciate the recent turn of events? Having skipped my gig in prison, why didn't I realize my good luck and simply get on with my life? Didn't the future present itself to me, as it did to her, in the shape of a question mark? And, who knows, maybe Promise was right. But mostly I was feeling low and lonely without my green notebooks, my illusions of novelistic grandeur, my rosary of words. Writing had been a torment, yes, but also a solace.

— —

Imagine for a moment that you're married, Promise said.

Married?

And then your wife dies. At first you mourn her death. You drag yourself to bars trying to meet new women, but really you're trying to find your dead wife. You know what I mean? And predictably none of the women are up to snuff. Or once or twice you make the mistake of thinking you've found a dead ringer for your wife, but it's only days before you're disillusioned. It's a predictable course of events, Evan. Then, after this period of mourning, you pursue other women, new women, different women, and you find yourself a wife, a wonderful wife, who's nothing like the wife you had. And yet—

Let me guess, I said. She's even better.

No, but she's—

Different, I said. Sorry, but no, I can't just sit down and start over. That novel is *gone.* And I can't get over the fact that everything I've ever written is currently ash.

I waited for her to respond. For a moment, I thought maybe the phone had gone dead; but no, it was only one of our silent periods—the kind that allowed me to think thoughts I didn't want to think. What was she really saying—not a better girlfriend, necessarily, but a new one?

They're only words, Promise finally said—her voice distant. The world is full of them.

— —

It didn't help that my conversations with Promise seemed different now, no longer whimsical. Things were much more serious. Almost exclusively now on the phone, we talked about what she called my *writing block,* what I chose to call my *predicament,* and the degree to which my despair was earned. Promise said my writing career was squarely in my own hands. In that moment I thought she was kidding, acting out a parody of glib advice, working the victim motif both ways. I did listen to her. I did take her advice seriously, and I set out numerous times to stick to a writing schedule. I even tried to imagine that little man up on my shoulder, egging me on. But I couldn't help thinking of Promise's optimism as an excuse for her pity.

Occasionally our conversations took on a lighter tone, but that was usually when we were talking about Bob. Both of us remained fascinated with the Partnow biography, if only because we had so little knowledge of recent developments. We speculated on the status of his career, the state of his mental health, the ins and outs of his love life. So far the media outlets had been stingy, telling us only that Bob had reappeared just as authorities had started to use the word *slim* to describe the chances that he was still alive.

— • —

First off, you aren't fickle.

Yes I am, Promise said—leaning against the refrigerator.

And I *do* appreciate what you've done for me. I'm sitting here in my own home, instead of some jail cell, and that's because of you. But you're also making me unhappy with all this talk of Hans and the sinus operation and going back to Manhattan. Aren't there any good vets here?

It's just—

Anyway, it's my fault, I said.

Hans's sinus infection?

No. The whole abduction thing.

You regret it?

Not exactly, I said. But I do regret it when I think of you, meeting you at the library, and how things might've been different. If I hadn't taken you down to the basement, if I hadn't abducted Bob in the first place.

But that's who you are, Evan.

Yes, that's me. A kidnapper at heart. A fuckup.

— • —

As the days passed, I felt myself drooping into a state of further despair. It made things worse that Promise had somehow resurrected her own confidence. She was writing up a storm. And she meant no offense when she told me that her Evan Ulmer had been freed from the tether of reality. Apparently, he was ascending just as I was sliding south.

Easy for you to say. These words, coming out of my mouth more than once during those weeks after Bob's departure, rubbed Promise the wrong way. She didn't like to hear me putting my plight in the context of her own writing career. (She never questioned that career, its future; she just didn't think it was useful to compare it to mine.) But there was some truth to the idea that things were easier for her—after all, she still had a novel to work on. I didn't.

Promise was writing a book about Evan Ulmer, but she'd given me red hair, involved me with an older woman, and probably jettisoned my nasty habit of clearing my throat. She hadn't made the mistake of rubbing shoulders with reality. She hadn't been so foolhardy as to take an experience—say, an abduction—and work it through the mill of her imagination until it came out the other side in a form barely, and badly, disguised. That was my particular forte—the autobiographical novel that begged others, the so-called characters, to intervene.

— —

Yes, that's me. A kidnapper at heart. A fuckup.

OK, you're a fuckup, Promise said. But I'm the fickle one.

You're *not* fickle. You just know when to move on. If I found out you were an ax murderer, I'd probably have second thoughts about you.

You're not an ax murderer, Evan.

I killed a dog.

It wasn't a dog, she said. It was a chihuahua.

— —

There *was* some good news. It became obvious that Bob wasn't going to betray me. According to murky accounts in the *Times,* the police had interviewed him for four hours. And apparently Bob denied that he'd been abducted and substituted, by way of explanation, what the police called "the equivalent of a nervous breakdown."

Promise told me that I should be flattered, that I'd obviously changed Bob's life. And gratified that Bob was keeping his promise. Instead, it shocked me how easily Bob could lie. Had he been lying, too, about liking my book?

— —

Is there ever a good way? Promise asked.

No. You're right. Of course there isn't.

Because if there is—

There isn't, I said—running a hand the length of Hans's spine and thinking of all the dogs I've stroked when really I've wanted to be touching their mistresses. Hans looked OK to me, despite the steady drip from his nose.

We were standing on my front porch, looking out on the neg-lected patch of grass that passed for my front yard. And no, Promise didn't want to come in. Was she just in the neighborhood? Had she dropped by to say good-bye? There was no suitcase dangling from her hand, but there might as well have been.

I could say I'm sorry, she said—tugging lightly on the leash, pulling Hans away from me. But that would be—

A mistake, I said—because I still liked finishing her sentences, even the ones that hurt.

When we hugged good-bye, I heard her cry. Softly, almost si-lently. But then she turned, Hans in tow, and so I never got a chance to see the tears. Would it have made a difference? Could I have cap-tured one of those tears, dropped it on a piece of paper, allowed it to dry, and then framed it and hung it over my bed to remind me that she'd felt *something*—not just indifference?

— —

I could've followed her. It wasn't entirely out of the question. A move to New York City wouldn't have been like getting on a Greyhound to follow your girl back to Wichita, Kansas. But I prided myself on being the kind of person who could take a hint. (With previous women, I was sometimes able to manufacture them out of thin air.) And I had to ask myself whether I wanted to return to the publishing capital, if not the literary center, of the entire country. Did I want to catch glimpses of attractive young people, Promise's contemporaries, sitting in cafes scribbling words into notebooks or typing them on laptops? With a pen no longer in my own hand, did I want to lower myself into the middle of that stew of ambition, only to sink fast and deep amid the buoyant?

— —

Did I try? Yes, I went out and bought a new green notebook, and a couple of times I went down to the library and took my usual seat at the usual table. Without Promise, of course. (To the librarians, I must've looked like half a person.) But the whole exercise was a waste of time.

On one of those futile trips, I picked up the next-to-most-recent *InStyle*—drawn to the picture of Scarlett Johansson on the cover; in turning its pages, I came across an article, "The Healing Power of Telling Stories," with a tagline about how more than a few celebrities had taken up the confessional pen. *Clinical research shows that long-buried traumas can depress the immune system, that old emotional wounds can continue to fester, and that writing about an experience— whether it took place yesterday or 30 years ago—can relieve stress and make us healthier.*

How very strange, to come across this article while flipping through a magazine in lieu of performing the painful task of writing. But soon this irony gave way to the realization that the most effective way to depress *my* immune system had always been a day of writing. Some men imagined themselves dying of a heart attack while screwing an exotic dancer in some dingy hotel; me, I always knew my heart would fail while I was deciding whether a comma or an em dash gave the appropriate illusion of pause. And reading this article at the library, I felt for perhaps the first time that it might be a good thing, even a healthy thing, *not* to write. Instead of seeing myself as a living embodiment of frustrated desire, a limp pen poised in my hand, I could choose to muzzle myself. I could be a little happy for once. And who knows, I might even be able to pick up the newest, hottest novel without that sickening feeling of envy.

— —

The story about Robert Partnow was in the *Times,* somewhat hidden on page B3. I would never have seen it if it hadn't been a slow news day, if I hadn't resorted to an article across the spread on corrupt transit officials.

I read this article, the one about Robert Partnow, the way a person might read his own obituary—slowly, word by word, my finger first hiding, and then revealing, the next line. It was the way I'd more than once imagined reading the first review of my first book.

Should I paraphrase the article?

— ·—

I felt a page turning—no small feat for a man who finds himself no longer a writer.

Each of us has our own way of initiating the process. It took me a good month to begin, but finally I was down there, taking things apart, getting rid of everything in the basement that reminded me of the abduction scenario. This dismantling of the paraphernalia of my crime was necessary, but it didn't really bring closure. What changed things for me was the acknowledgment—fueled by late-afternoon martinis—that my life could never be the same. No sense pining for the past. Maybe I'd lost a limb, but hadn't I also gained a leg up on my previous self—the one forever in need of literary success or religion or the right girl? *You can dress him up,* my father used to say, *but can you take him out?* Another of his front-loaded questions; and yet hadn't I always made that same mistake—thinking of myself as a recipe missing a key ingredient?

It certainly wasn't the first time in my life that I tried to take on a fresh perspective. But things *did* look slightly different now, even on the grander scale of tabloid news. We were in the headlines again, Bob and me. I'd been sacrificed to the larger good of the story, but without suffering the indignity of prison. We'd been retrieved from the wastepaper basket of yesterday's news, and I liked the idea of a story having lost its own legs and then regained them. *Robert Partnow is alive!* Not that there wasn't something egotistical even in this—my continued interest in Bob and the idea of the abduction scenario getting him over the hump of professional malaise.

—·—

Should I paraphrase the article? No, it's probably better to reproduce it in its entirety.

In a surprising twist to the story of the publishing editor who went missing for over six weeks before he walked into a mid-Manhattan police station on 18 May, Robert Partnow is now telling law-enforcement authorities that he has written a book. Claiming to have been inspired by press coverage of his own disappearance, Mr. Partnow has written a novel, tentatively titled "Tearjerker," which outlines the bizarre tale of an intense relationship between a failed writer and an editor very much like Mr. Partnow.

"From what we now know, Mr. Partnow didn't in fact suffer a nervous breakdown but took off for a period of time in order to write a novel," says John Mulcahy, a spokesperson for the NYPD. According to police, who have seen the manuscript, Mr. Partnow's story is a first-person narrative about a man who, frustrated by his own career and his lack of success, kidnaps a fiction editor and then releases him after forty-five days—the exact number of days that Mr. Partnow was declared missing.

"Robert Partnow is embarrassed by the details of his own disappearance and sorry for any pain he has caused loved ones, as well as for any expenses he has caused the City of New York," according to a statement released by Robert Cohen, Mr. Partnow's attorney. "He is also regretful for constructing the original story of suffering a 'nervous breakdown,' which was a falsehood." According to Mr. Cohen, more details about the novel and Mr. Partnow's plans for the future will be disclosed soon, once any legal repercussions have been dealt with.

Some colleagues in the publishing industry appeared stupe-

fied upon hearing that Mr. Partnow had disappeared to write a novel. One editor, asking not to be identified, speculated that Mr. Partnow might have suffered a life crisis, if not a nervous break-down, and written the novel to climb out of a depression.

Mr. Partnow would not be the first publishing executive to have authorial aspirations, let alone success. Michael Korda, editor in chief of Simon & Schuster, is the author of many books. Before pub-lishing a string of successful novels, Pulitzer Prize–winner Toni Morrison worked as an editor for ten years.

I reread the article a few times, top to bottom, if only to stop myself from thinking too much. I read it so intently that I probably could've repeated the article from memory, like some schoolboy reciting a Longfellow poem at the front of the class.

Finally, my fingers blackened from the newsprint, I let it go—the newspaper falling to my feet. I let pretty much *everything* go. My mind raced, and thoughts ran pell-mell toward anger. I hated Bob, that cocksucker, for what he had done, for what he was doing. I'd call the *Times* and reveal the truth, give myself up, go to prison for the sake of literary integrity. But I couldn't do that. Not now. Not when the book was finally getting its shot, finding an audience. And Bob knew this. He knew that I wouldn't make a stink, that I couldn't, and he'd used that against me.

Even if I had to tip my hat to his genius, his gumption, the way he'd put together a nice little package of deceit, I hated his title. *Tearjerker?* What was Bob thinking? Was he being ironic? Was he obliquely trying to mask the sentimental aspects of the story, and particularly its ending?

—◆—

Do you have any retail experience?

No, I said.

But you *are* a reader, Betty Wilcox said—smiling, feeding me a line, suggesting the right response to her own question. We've certainly seen you here on more than one occasion. You *are* a customer.

I had to think hard to remember if that was true, whether I'd ever actually made a purchase at Booknook. But it didn't matter. In fact, nothing seemed to matter—my inept if honest answers to her questions were repeatedly swept to the side, as though providence was working its magic behind the scenes. Apparently, destiny had me firmly by the lapels. And Ms. Wilcox, with her intense blue eyes, had an opening.

I knew what Promise would say. She would scoff at the idea of taking a job at Booknook—she'd tell me I was wasting my time, throwing away my talent on a third-rate bookstore.

OK, it *was* somewhat depressing, but Booknook wasn't that bad.

— —

Did she know? Had she known? Had she known without knowing? Did she not want to know? These were the questions that knocked at the thin, hollow door to my heart. And I had no answers. If you were to place a gun to my temple, I suspect I'd say that she *didn't* know. Promise had no idea. She'd negotiated my freedom in good faith. She'd assumed the best of Bob, taken him at his word. And yet I did have my suspicions—that Promise *did* know, in her own intuitive way, and that Bob would never have promised anything to a temperamental twenty-five-year-old.

Promise was home now, living with her parents (*temporarily,* she'd insisted the day she left—I had my suspicions about that, too); and yes, there were phone calls, or at least messages on my machine, proclaiming her surprise, telling me that she'd known nothing, expressing her most sincere condolences. I never returned those calls, even though I worried that not returning them might suggest to Promise that I somehow held her responsible. I didn't.

— —

Bored, I did it on a whim. One day, a month or so after Promise had gone off with her dog and returned to Manhattan, I cleaned out the utility drawer in the kitchen. I rounded up stray paper clips, depleted ballpoint pens, takeout menus, unclassifiable food particles. And at the back of the drawer I came upon a very small piece of paper, folded three times into a perfect little square. Opening it, I felt transported to some proverbial beach—toes sunk in wet sand, pants rolled halfway up my calves, heavy beard covering my face. It was a message from a bottle, with handwriting that consigned to me both the pride and the chagrin of authorship.

I think it is about longing for the unattainable poetically perfect woman. She is far away and better than me and contact with her will transform me into a me that is not only better but somehow different—not the real me but an imagined me. In my case, this imagined me may be called "a genius," the ever-so-talented producer at ease with himself and confident and at ease with producing greatness without effort, all by being merged with the long-sought-after woman.

There was something remarkably innocent about it—the raw handwriting, the unrevised syntax, the bare emotion of wanting something so badly that you'd busy yourself in whipping off an analysis on a torn piece of paper. The paper itself—white, blue-lined, like a schoolboy's—only enhanced the aura of innocence. Where exactly had I penned this ode to perfection, this hard slap of reality on my own cheek? Not in Sandhurst. Was it back when I was living on Houston Street, during those days of hopelessness? Did I write it at a cafe, sans green notebook, while looking at an *unattainable poetically perfect woman* sitting at an adjacent table? Had I inadvertently transferred this written crumb to some random box that I tossed into the U-Haul?

I stared at the creased paper—a miniature accordion in the grasp of my thumbs and forefingers—and thought of Promise and Bob. And yes, I thought of them *together*. Maybe not in a romantic sense, but as a package—heavy baggage inside my head. (They were like parents in that sense.) For a few splendid weeks, Promise and Bob had transformed me into a better me; even if, in the end, they'd left me with this sad note to myself as the only written relic, of a personal nature, that I possessed. Which raised the question: How much *me* could there be without any words? As if to find out, I balled up the scrap of paper and tossed it in the trash can under the sink.

— —

I hadn't been watching a lot of television, so it was a matter of pure chance. That night in my bedroom, I was changing channels and suddenly there he was—Robert Partnow, ex-editor, first novelist, sitting across the table from Charlie Rose.

As it happened, I only caught the last minute or so of his segment; all too quickly, after a ten-second break, Bob was magically replaced at the table by Russell Crowe, which hardly seemed fair. (All that hair, for one thing.) And so I'd barely managed to get a glimpse of Bob, looking literary in a buttoned-down white shirt, smiling as Rose stumbled his way, unctuously, vaguely in the direction of a concluding thought. *And we do look forward. To this book, this novel,* Tearjerker, *soon to be available. In bookstores. Thank you, Robert Partnow, for being here.*

At noon the next day *The Charlie Rose Show* was rebroadcast, and so I watched the entire segment. I was happy to see that Bob looked as though he'd kept the weight off—in fact, he might have lost a few additional pounds. He'd cut his hair very short, which somehow created a more youthful impression. (Styling advice from Claudia, or the irrepressible Lloyd?) He was quite eloquent, really—sitting there at the big round wooden table, a glass of water at the ready, speaking his mind about the state of contemporary fiction and expressing empathy for writers who, like his protagonist, failed to make the grade. He himself had known failure, he said—not as an editor, but, during an earlier period of his life, as an aspiring writer. Bob did hedge a little when he was asked about his so-called disappearance; he appeared defensive as he talked about his exact whereabouts, his daily writing habits, his influences, and so on. But Charlie Rose, pleased that he had nabbed a luminary for his first on-camera interview, let him off easy—returning to the important topic of his forthcoming book.

Sitting there in my bedroom watching this was, as you might imagine, an unnerving experience. The most peculiar thing, though, was that I felt OK about watching Bob doing this interview—the one I'd imagined, for myself, more than a few times. He was better than I would've been, there was little doubt about that. And it struck me, listening to Bob, that he *was* telling the truth, even if it used to be my truth and not his. Bob was playing the role of Evan Ulmer and doing a more-than-competent job.

OK, it *was* somewhat depressing, but Booknook wasn't that bad. A few too many books on yoga and other pursuits of a spiritual nature, and far too many titles in the self-help section. There were two shelves next to the spinning rack of maps filled with travel guides to the Hudson Valley. Too many mothers came in with small children and spoke in loud, singsong voices to their strollered captives. And yet not everything testified to the death of culture. There was a table near the entrance with the newest fiction prominently displayed. I imagined that one day soon Bob's book, our book, would be there, several copies in a neat rectangular stack among that smorgasbord of the latest—*Tearjerker,* in all its clothbound glory. (Come to think of it, that title was sort of growing on me.) And maybe Betty would ask me to write up one of the little tentlike index cards that sat next to our "Booknook Favorites." *Set in our own wonderful town of Sandhurst, this quirky novel tells the story of a failed writer and his desperate quest for fame.*

Here's how it works: you decide you're going to do something really, really outrageous. Imagine, if you will, abducting an editor at a major publishing house and keeping him in your basement for forty-five days. And you think this might change literary history, cause a slight ripple on the world's gentle surface, or at least force the hand of the Library of Congress. Yes, a book, *yours*—a *raison d'être,* an excuse for a life. If nothing else, you'll end up in prison, on the receiving end of interactions with thugs and worse.

But it doesn't happen that way. Or it *didn't.* Instead, weeks passed. I became adept at chitchatting with Booknook customers and fishing change from the cash register; a publication date was announced and copies of *Tearjerker* were slated for arrival in bookstores, my name absent from the spines and dust jackets manufactured somewhere in deep Kentucky. Meanwhile, my once-in-a-while girlfriend who'd seen the light and returned to sane alternatives now led a mysterious life in an exciting city. Kisses took on a new role as fodder for my memories. And after the dust settled, it was just me and my gun.

Yes, of course—I kept the gun.

— —

One night, as I lay in bed, I closed my eyes and spun a series of fantasies about *Tearjerker,* its appearance in Booknook and everywhere else, and the kind of celebrity that Bob might eventually achieve. (Silly to say, but I felt giddy—like at the beginning of a romance; maybe it had to do with confidences held between two people.) Soon he'd be giving readings with other heavyweight authors at the New York Public Library. He'd probably be going away for stints at Yaddo and the MacDowell Colony, where he'd meet and sleep with impressionable young poets—male and female. And fiction writers, occasionally. Who knows, in time he might meet up with Promise. Stranger things had happened.

— —

Yes, of course—I kept the gun. I took the Porta-Potty to the county dump, I donated the bunk beds to the Salvation Army and the chain-link fence to the elementary school down the road. I sold the treadmill for $525 on eBay to a rabbi in Queens. But I kept the gun. (I'm grateful to Bob for returning it, and I choose to believe that his generosity wasn't a nudge toward self-punishment.) I've thought once or twice of getting rid of it. But what's the use? It is, come to think of it, the only remnant I have of the abduction scenario, of those deliciously nerve-racking days of drama and inspiration.

There are still evenings—after I return from a day of work at Booknook, after dinner and the national news—when I take the gun and go for walks. In these days of summer, I wear my light cotton jacket to conceal the weapon. I walk through the neighborhood and look into people's windows, calmed by flickering televisions and covetous of all the characters beyond my control. (The real people, I mean, not the people on television.) Sometimes I pass Promise's house, count the weeds, open the alligator-cum-mailbox, awash in purple and green, and rifle through correspondence waiting for a more sympathetic reader.

Staring into my neighbors' homes, at the shadows of their fleeting movements, I've often thought about how everyone has a secret life. I have my gun, but I'm hardly alone. And sometimes our indiscretions *do* get shared. (What use are secrets if you can't give one away occasionally?) Take, for instance, Bob and me—we share a secret and always will. We made one up, over the course of a few weeks in April and May, even if we had no idea that that's what we were doing. And I know Bob thinks of me, if only because of this secret. In between appearances on talk shows and readings in cities he'd rather not visit, he'll remember me—my round face, my green notebooks, my throat and its fastidious imperatives.

I've thought about writing to Bob, saying hi, congratulations, whatever. Thought about it a lot. Setting aside the potential for perilous repercussions, though, I always conclude that I don't have anything to say—nothing notable, startling, trenchant. I'm no longer a writer, really, even though I do sometimes jot a line or two, to myself, in one of my green notebooks. But nowadays whatever I might say has already been said by someone else, and so it doesn't need to be said again. Anyway, Bob knows how I feel. And, at the risk of being presumptuous—I know how he feels, too. I do.

DANIEL HAYES is the author of *Kissing You,* a collection of short stories. He lives in San Francisco, California. Visit his web site at www.hayestearjerker.com.

Tearjerker has been typeset in Galliard, a typeface designed by Matthew Carter who based it on the designs of the sixteenth-century French typecutter Robert Granjon.

Book design by Wendy Holdman.
Composition by Stanton Publication Services, Inc., St. Paul.
Manufactured by Friesens on acid-free paper.